Gravity Falls

Dipper and Mabel

AND THE CURSE OF THE TIME PIRATES' TREASURE!

A "Select Your Own Choose-Venture!"

Written by Jeffrey Rowe
Additional Story by Alex Hirsch
Art by Emmy Cicierega
Editorial by Eric Geron
Design by Lindsay Broderick
Based on the series created by Alex Hirsch

DISNEY PRESS

Los Angeles • New York

Printed in the United States of America
First Hardcover Edition, July 2016
9 10
FAC-008598-21302
Library of Congress Control Number: 2015946655
ISBN 978-1-4847-4668-4

For more Disney Press fun, visit www.disneybooks.com

SUSTAINABLE
FORESTRY
INITIATIVE

Certified Sourcing
www.sfiprogram.org
SFI-01268

Logo Applies to Text Stock Only

Hello there, dear reader!

What you hold in your hands is not an ordinary book. This book is an adventure, one in which every decision is made by you! Or by your pushy friend, if he or she happens to be reading over your shoulder. I hate when people do that. I'm talking to you, Steve.

Our characters have a perilous journey ahead, and it's up to you to make the right calls to send them to a happy ending or to a horrifying fate. If you do end up casting Dipper, Mabel, and Blendin into a wormhole, don't feel too bad. You can always use a form of time travel known as "flipping back through pages" to try again. With enough good sense and luck, you may find the coveted Time Pirates' Treasure! For your sake, I hope you do, because the friend reading over your shoulder will probably make fun of you if you fail. Steve is such a jerk sometimes. Thinks he's better than me just because his dad owns a yacht. Good luck making the right choices . . . if you dare!

Sincerely,
Omniscient Nameless Narrator

INTRODUCTION

It's another usually unusual day in Gravity Falls! The green grass rustles in a breeze; the sun shines down through the trees; and a pair of familiar twins strolls through the forest. As usual, they're in the middle of an argument.

"It doesn't matter," says Dipper Pines. "Just pick one already!"

"Yes, it DOES matter," says Mabel Pines, holding two sweaters in her hands. "The sweater I wear has to match the day perfectly! It's sunny, so I feel like wearing my 'Puppy with Shades' sweater. But I've also got a really good feeling about this 'Glittering Yarn Ball' sweater."

"Little choices like this aren't important," says Dipper. "That's why I wear the same outfit every day, so I can focus on BIG choices."

"And everyone else can focus on trying to ignore how bad you smell!" laughs Mabel. After pondering seriously, she finally puts on the yarn ball sweater, tossing the other aside. "I think I'm gonna go with 'Yarn Ball' today," she says. "I wore a dog sweater yesterday and I don't want people to think I'm getting predictable."

Dipper throws an arm out and stops Mabel in her tracks. "Do you hear that?" he asks.

Mabel looks around. "Is it the sound of fashion lovers everywhere applauding my sweater decision?"

Dipper frowns. "It sounds like . . . digging." He leads Mabel up a mossy hill. They peer over it just as . . .

SMACK!

"Aw, time-dangit!" says a portly man in a gray jumpsuit and goggles who just smacked himself in the face with his shovel. He stands in the middle of a clearing, surrounded by nearly a hundred shallow holes.

"Blendin Blandin!" shouts Mabel, beaming.

"Who goes there!" Blendin shrieks, wielding his shovel like a sword. "I have various futuristic weapons and I will attempt to figure out how to use them if you get closer!" he shouts.

Dipper and Mabel laugh and slide down the hill.

"Hey, buddy. How are you?" says Dipper.

"How's the new hair working out?" asks Mabel.

"YOU TWO!" says Blendin. "I should have known. I'll have you know my business is personal!"

"Sure are a lot of holes here," says Dipper.

"Hundreds of holes," says Mabel.

"What's with the holes?" asks Dipper.

"Are you looking for gophers?" asks Mabel. "Because that's adorable and we want in!"

Blendin blots his brow. "What I'm doing is a secret!" he says, scowling before accidentally hitting himself in the face with the shovel again. He grumbles and breaks his shovel over his knee. "Fine, I'll tell you, but only because I need help! I'm looking for a buried treasure hidden by a madman. This treasure is so large and powerful that the kindest of souls have made ghosts of their enemies to get it!"

"Is the treasure friendship?" asks Mabel.

"No, it isn't friendship!" screams Blendin. "I'm talking about the legendary TIME PIRATES' TREASURE!"

"Ooooooooooh," says Mabel.

"It's the greatest treasure ever known, because it's EVERY great treasure ever known. The Time Pirates are a group of rogue Time Anomaly Enforcement Agents who travel through history and steal the world's most famous treasures. The Holy Grail! The Philosopher's Stone! Abraham Lincoln's pet dodo! And they dress like pirates because . . . it looks cool!"

"That's debatable," says Dipper.

"Hey! They're the most feared and respected group of rapscallions to ever exist!" says Blendin. "And I've found a way to steal their most precious possessions!"

"Stealing from bloodthirsty pirates seems kind of dangerous," Dipper says. "I thought you hated danger. And doing things."

"Look," sighs Blendin. "I don't know if you know this, but my life isn't exactly great. Even though you got me my old job back, I live with my mom, my coworkers still make fun of me, and I'm so stressed my new hair keeps falling out." Blendin pulls out a clump of hair and scatters it to the winds. "If I could take even one-quarter of that treasure, I could finally get the respect I need. But I can't do it alone, if you haven't noticed." Blendin motions to the field of holes. "So what do you say? Help me thieve from these thieves?"

"I dunno," says Dipper. "We were going to watch TV all day."

"Or read a book," says Mabel. "I heard someone on TV say that they still make books."

"We could split the treasure three ways!" says Blendin, smiling. "That's more than a million dollars each!"

"But isn't time travel super dangerous?" asks Dipper. "What if I step on a twig and create a future where everyone turns into lizard people?"

"The lizard people scenario happens only forty percent of the time," says Blendin. "And they're usually pretty nice. Plus, I brought some laser blasters to keep us safe! Look!" Blendin whips out one of the strange time-travel weapons and fires it into the forest. They hear what sounds like Toby

Determined screaming in the distance. "See?" Blendin says. "Works like a charm!"

Dipper and Mabel look at each other, nod, and huddle up.

"Mabel, a lot of treasure could be cool," Dipper whispers.

"Yeah! I could use it to buy Moon Shoes or gild Waddles in solid gold!" says Mabel.

"And I could build my own laboratory to study the weirdness of Gravity Falls! And possibly get a few hundred pairs of the exact same outfit to wear!" Dipper glances up at Blendin, who's watching them from a distance, then back at Mabel. "So what do we do, Mabel? Should we help Blendin out?"

Reader, what should Dipper and Mabel do?

DECLINE BLENDIN'S OFFER:
GO TO PAGE 71

GO AFTER THE TREASURE:
GO TO PAGE 103

SLAY THE DRAGON

"**D**RAGONS!" says Dipper, pulling Journal 3 from his vest. "I've uncovered some of their bones back in Gravity Falls, but I've never been able to see one live. This is the opportunity of a lifetime!"

"Aren't dragons basically just talking dinosaurs?" asks Mabel.

"The science is still out on that," says Dipper.

"Veeeeryyyy good!" squeals the king. "Sir Suitsly, equip them with armor!"

A bespectacled old tailor hobbles out, measures the trio, and then claps his hands, summoning two squires, who secure armor on the twins and Blendin. With expert hands, the tailor carves customized symbols onto their breastplates.

"Mine is an hourglass!" says Blendin. "It's perfect!"

"And mine is a shooting star!" says Mabel.

"Hey, mine is a pine tree!" says Dipper.

"Don't get too excited," says the king. "These are only to make it easier to identify your bodies after you've been killed."

Blendin frowns.

"Squire, present them with the dragon flute!" says the king.

A squire boy prances out with a wooden box and opens

it. Inside is a wooden fife with a dragon carved on it.

"This is a dragon flute," says the king. "Playing a note from it will lull any dragon to sleep!"

"If it's that easy, why haven't you used it yourself?" asks Dipper.

"Because I have no idea if it actually works!" says the king. "You think I'm actually dumb enough to risk my life trying it?"

He cackles as a squire hands them their swords.

Dipper hands one to Mabel and one to Blendin.

"And here's a map of the dragon's den," says the king, handing Dipper a scroll of parchment. "Now, now, I'll tell you all about that pirate person you speak of and his key only after you've returned. Off you go! Tee-hee!"

A cadre of knights escorts the trio out of the castle.

"The dragon's that way," grumbles a knight, pointing off into the hills beyond the village. "Good luck." He hands them a torch, laughs, and slams the castle doors behind them.

"Well, it looks like it's quest time!" says Dipper.

Mabel grabs a lute from a plague-ridden peasant lying facedown in the mud. As they make their way to the forest, she begins to sing:

Oh, harken ye close, that you may hear the fable!
Of a dragon defeater named Marvelous Mabel!
She traveled the land, so the legend is heard!
With Blendin the Bald and Dipper the Nerd.

"Someone take that thing away from her," grumbles Dipper.

✦ ✦✦ ✦

Thirteen verses later, the trio has traveled over glen and dale and reaches the den of the dragon.

"*With her glittery sword, she defeated the beast! And then married thirteen hot princes at least!*" sings Mabel.

"Shhh!" whispers Dipper, sweeping his torch in front of him.

Human bones are strewn around the dark cavern, and sharp craggy stalactites hang like crooked teeth at the threshold. From inside comes the thunderous echo of the dragon's breathing. It shakes the earth beneath the gang's feet.

"All right, we just need to sneak in and play this dragon flute," says Dipper. "Hopefully we can lull it to sleep before it incinerates us, and then steal back the king's favorite goblet. Plus, I might take a few scales back home to brag to Soos."

"Who needs dragon scales when we'll have a whole treasure to bring back?" says Mabel.

"Uhhh, is everyone else s-super cool with this p-plan?" stammers Blendin, his armor clanking as his knees tremble and knock together. "The crushed skulls and rib cages around the cave are giving me sort of an iffy vibe."

Dipper looks at the king's map. "Well, according to this map, there's an alternate cliff we could take to a back entrance to the cave," he says, gesturing to a thin, crumbling precipice precariously wrapping around the mountain high in the air.

Blendin gulps. "Oh, man, things are getting iffier and iffier."

"Hey, the choice is yours," says Dipper. "You wanna take the dangerous cliff and sneak up from the back? Or burst in the front and hope this dragon flute works?"

Blendin grunts. "I hate making decisions."

Luckily, reader, he has you to make the decision for him.

CONFRONT THE DRAGON WITH THE FLUTE: GO TO PAGE 187

SNEAK UP ON THE DRAGON FROM THE BACK: GO TO PAGE 154

EXPLODE THE BOOSTERS

"**I**'m exploding the boosters!" says Mabel. "This button's big and red, and that's always a good thing! Three . . . two . . . one!" She slams her palm on the button.

For a moment, nothing seems to happen, and then all of a sudden—

BOOOOOOSH!

With a force greater than anything they've ever experienced before, their racer rockets forward. The g-forces are so intense that Dipper and Mabel struggle to hold on to their seats. With a sonic boom, they speed past *Racer T* and cross the finish line.

"We won!" screams Mabel.

"We did it!" shouts Dipper.

The crowd goes wild.

Blendin stumbles out of the stands and rushes down to meet the twins. "W-w-w-way to go, guys, that was really amazing! I've seen a lot of space races in my life, but that was really something else!" he yells, hugging them.

The twins struggle for air.

"I want you guys to meet someone," says Blendin, releasing them. "Dipper and Mabel, this is the ex-Time Pirate we've won the freedom of, Dos Hunthou!"

Dos Hunthou, the buff, shirtless convict with the time scar, runs up to the twins like an eager puppy.

"Master, mastress, what is your bidding?" asks Dos Hunthou with a bow.

The Time Key falls from the shackle around his neck, dangling on a chain.

"Do a funny dance!" yells Mabel. "There better be kicks!"

Dos Hunthou starts to rush off to obey.

"Wait!" says Dipper. "We're actually here to set you free. If you give us that key you wear around your neck, you have your freedom!"

Dos Hunthou looks down at his key.

"This key? But of course!" He hands the key to Dipper.

"Yes!" says Dipper.

"Now tell me, master, what is your bidding?" asks Dos Hunthou.

"Uh, dude, I'm not your master," says Dipper. "You're free now. Go be free!"

"Giving me my freedom is the kindest thing anyone's ever done! I am eternally in your debt! I will wait on you hand and foot for all time!" says Dos Hunthou.

Dipper scratches his head. "You realize you're leaving one prison for another, right?" he asks.

Dos Hunthou looks at him blankly.

Dipper pulls Mabel and Blendin aside. "Guys," he says, "I don't know what to do about this. It's not like we can take him along with us. . . ."

"Can't we just leave him on the side of the road with a twenty-dollar bill stapled to his neck shackle?" asks Mabel.

"I wish, but it's very dishonorable to him!" says Blendin. "He'll have to live the rest of his life in shame! We either have to take him on as our sacred helper or pass him on to someone in need. Which should we do?"

The twins look at each other and shrug.

A fly lands on Dos Hunthou's eye.

He doesn't swat it away.

"What do we do, Mabel?" asks Dipper.

GIVE DOS HUNTHOU TO SOMEONE IN NEED: GO TO PAGE 252

ACCEPT DOS HUNTHOU AS THEIR OWN: GO TO PAGE 64

FUTURE PRISON BREAK

"**L**et's break into time prison!" says Mabel. "I hear it's a . . . riot! Huh? *Huh?*" Mabel elbows Blendin in the side.

"Listen, Mabel, the Infinitentiary is no joke!" yells Blendin. "I was in that death trap for one thousand years. Or maybe two years. I'm a really bad judge of time. That's probably why I get fired so often from my time job."

Dipper and Mabel roll their eyes.

"The bottom line is," says Blendin, "between the time gangs and the hover rats, we've got our work cut out for us here. But Davy Time-Jones is in that prison with our answers, and if we want to get him out, we have to get ourselves in first. Any ideas?"

"Okay," says Dipper, pacing. "I've got a plan. The first thing we have to do is pick out some criminals who are wanted fugitives. We'll spend a year studying their mannerisms and lifestyles, getting to know them as well as we know ourselves. Then, with the aid of a world-class surgeon and classified military technology, we'll switch our faces with theirs, go into the prison, and impersonate them. After several months of gaining the inmates' trust, and proving that we're dangerous criminals by then, we'll escape with their secrets. But! When we return to the real world, we'll discover that the criminals we've impersonated have taken *our* faces, and we may need to have some sort of legendary showdown with them, and there'll probably be doves. There are always doves."

Mabel snorts and laughs. "Bro, you're forgetting what Grunkle Stan says. Getting into prison is easy! Here, watch this!" Mabel spies a policeman walking by and tugs his shirt. "Excuse me, we'd like to confess to time crimes!"

"Which ones?" asks the police officer.

"All of them," says Mabel. "All of the time crimes."

"Time larceny?" asks the officer.

"Yup," says Mabel.

"Clock theft?"

"Yes!"

"Time-icide?"

"Totally!"

"Indecent clock-sposure?"

"Absolutely."

"Vehicular time-slaughter?"

"That, too!"

"Disorderly chrono-duct?"

"Uhmmm-hmmm!"

"Time forgery?"

"You know it!"

"Time laundering?"

"Uh-huh!"

"Minute trafficking?"

"All day, every day!"

"Future arson?"

"Extra that, please!"

"Time-bezzlement?"

"Totally!"

"Really? Time-bezzlement?" he asks.

"We time-bezzled the whoa out of some people," she says.

The police officer stares at Mabel, Dipper, and Blendin. "Well, you three are clearly the most ruthless criminals I've ever met. Better send you to prison for infinity!" He pulls out his handcuffs.

"Yay!" the three cheer in unison.

The police officer takes the gang to a futuristic police station. He makes them swap their clothes for striped jumpsuits, and the officers take Blendin's laser blasters, too.

"Oooh! These prison jumpsuits are surprisingly comfortable," says Mabel, smoothing hers out.

"It's the future!" says Blendin. "Everything is made of spandex! Clothes, chairs, even celebrities."

The twins rub their arms to feel the spandex's softness, oohing and aahing.

"Please stop enjoying your prison clothes," snaps the guard.

Dipper and Mabel frown.

Moments later, Dipper, Mabel, and Blendin are thrust into the back of a hovering squad car. Within seconds, they've passed through the stratosphere and are docking at an enormous space station in the shape of an infinity symbol. A floating sign reads:

THE INFINITENTIARY: YOUR TIME IS UP

"Welcome to the Infinitentiary. First stop: cafeteria."

A door opens before the trio, and they find themselves face to face with a scene of utter chaos: hundreds of strange convicts, aliens, and rogues are engaged in an all-out food fight. One beats another over the head with a clock, takes his steamed cabbage, and shoves it down a third one's throat.

"What's going on?" shouts Dipper.

"Gang fight," says the guard. "This prison is ruled by two warring gangs. Frankly, I don't understand why they can't just get along. Might be the time madness. Anyway, good luck staying alive." The guard closes the door and seals the air ducts behind them.

The twins and Blendin stare at the melee. A half man, half bird screeches above the room, dumping mustard on a group of toasters in striped pajamas. A large one-eyed human catapults mashed potatoes with a spoon.

Dipper, Mabel, and Blendin back up against the wall.

"*Gleeee glor!*" screams a chameleon man who is blending in with the wall. "*Gleem glop glop!*" He pushes

the trio away from him and toward the center of the room.

"What do we do?" asks Mabel. She ducks to avoid a wayward pie. "I'm no good in food fights! I always want to eat my weapon!"

"I don't know!" yells Blendin. "I never joined a gang! I usually hide in the corner and try to blend in with the whitest surface I can find!"

A large bearded and tattooed convict approaches the twins and Blendin. He has an eye patch and a tattoo of a skull and crossbones on his shoulder. He cocks back a bowl of chili to throw at them.

"I'm Davy Time-Jones and I ain't ever seen you before," he growls. "What side are you on? Are you a Clock King or a Time Duke?" he asks, wild-eyed. "'Cause depending on your answer, you're either my sworn brothers or my worst enemies."

Mabel blurts, "Uh . . . uh . . . Blendin knows!"
Blendin blurts, "Uh . . . uh . . . Dipper knows!"
Dipper blurts, "Uh . . . uh . . . We're the . . ."

TIME DUKES: GO TO PAGE 249
CLOCK KINGS: GO TO PAGE 274

JOUST AGAINST HIM

"**I** choose . . . JOUSTING!" **Dipper says,** stepping forward.

Mabel's and Blendin's jaws drop.

"Wait, what?" yells Mabel. *"Jousting?"*

"Wait, I meant to say chess," says Dipper. "I said chess, right?"

Mabel shakes her head at Dipper.

"Woo, that was not a good slip of the tongue," Dipper says.

"So be it!" declares the king with a clap of his hands.

A squire straps armor on Dipper and puts him on the back of a horse.

"So, uh, dude, do you have any tips?" asks Dipper.

"Hit him with the pointy end," says the squire. "And do it first."

Dipper gulps.

Moments later, the king on his golden balcony throne looks out over the jousting field, a huge arena decked out with multicolored tapestries depicting the heroic deaths of past failed jousters. Mabel and Blendin stand beside him. Down below, a chicken in a striped tunic with *Referee* stitched on it pecks at the ground. Dipper rides his horse out onto the jousting field, and the crowd cheers.

"Seriously, guys, I really meant ch-chess," Dipper

stammers. "Are you really going to let a child joust a full-grown man?"

Trumpets announce Sir Swollsley's arrival.

"YES-ith! YES-ith! Gazeth upon my pipes!" Swollsley yells, flexing his arms.

"When the trumpet blasts, ye shall charge and try to dismount each other!" the king shouts out to the contestants. "Whoever is left upright shall be the victor!"

"Yeah, bro, I love that! I LOVE THAT!" screams Swollsley.

"But whoever loses will be remembered in one of our lovely death tapestries, now available for sale in our Gift Shoppe!" shouts the king.

Dipper gulps, lowers his visor, and attempts to focus. He locks eyes on Swollsley, who's kissing his lance and biceps.

The trumpet sounds.

Dipper and Swollsley charge, racing at each other with dangerous speed. Dipper bounces up and down on his horse, barely able to hold the lance straight. Right as he is in striking range, Dipper closes his eyes and—

SMACK!

Dipper opens his eyes. He's still upright on his horse. He looks back and sees he has successfully dismounted his opponent.

"Incredible!" shouts Mabel from the stands. "Dipper's so short, Swollsley's lance went right over him!"

"NO! THIS IS NOT RIGHT, BRO!" yells the vanquished knight.

"Woo!" screams Dipper, tossing back his visor and grinning.

"Yippee!" squeals the king, clapping madly.

"Woo-hoo! Can a sister get her key now?" asks Mabel.

"Ho-ho-ho! Goodness, no. Not until Dipper takes my daughter's hand in marriage!" says the king. "That's the whole reason we're doing this, remember?"

"Wait, *what*?" says Dipper.

"A wedding! This is so exciting!" Mabel squeals.

"What, Mabel?" says Dipper. "I don't wanna get married!"

"Oh, you better," says the king. "It would be a great insult to me if you didn't. You're marrying this girl, finding a replacement suitor, or facing the consequences of defying the king!" His knights surround Dipper, their spearheads aimed right at him.

The chicken referee seems to have no opinion on the matter.

"What'll it be, boy?" asks the king.

Dipper's in some real hot soup now, I tell ya!

ACCEPT THE MARRIAGE: GO TO PAGE 112

FIND A REPLACEMENT SUITOR: GO TO PAGE 23

REFUSE TO MARRY THE KING'S DAUGHTER: GO TO PAGE 82

FIND A REPLACEMENT SUITOR

"**Okay, okay, I know this sounds crazy,**" Dipper tells the king, "but I'm not super into getting married, and you really want someone to marry your daughter, so what if I find a replacement suitor? Like a totally eligible bachelor who could really use the romance connection, and then you can marry your daughter to him and we can go on our way!"

The king strokes his beard. "How long will this process take?"

"Literally a second!" says Dipper. He grabs the time tape out of Blendin's hand, pulls it, and whooshes out of sight. Exactly one second later, with a triumphant flash of light, Dipper returns with a familiar bachelor.

"Hey! Get your hands off me, dork!" says Robbie, stumbling to the ground. "What? *Where are we?* Is this Amish country or something?"

"You are in my court, young squire, here to marry my daughter!" says the king.

Robbie looks at Dipper. "Is he for real?"

Dipper nods.

"Score!" says Robbie with a fist pump. "A dark Gothic castle. Royalty. A pretty maiden—wait, she's pretty, right?"

The king claps his hands, and out walks a redheaded girl. "I present to you my daughter, Wendinella!" says the king.

She looks exactly like Wendy.

"'Sup, dude?" she says.

Robbie pumps his fist again. Then he grabs a lute from a squire and plucks out a melody.

"Dude, you play the lute? No way!" says Wendinella. "I've always wanted to date a musician."

"Well, now you get to marry one, baby," says Robbie with a smirk.

Wendinella bats her eyelashes at him.

Dipper smacks himself in the face.

"Ha! Bet you wish you didn't make that choice!" says Mabel.

"We can go back and undo this, *right*?" says Dipper.

"Hey, where's the time tape?" Dipper sees that Robbie has grabbed the time tape and is spinning it on his finger.

"Guess you won't need this anymore!" says Robbie, chucking it on the ground and shattering it into a hundred tiny pieces. "Hey, what are you three slave-dorks looking at? To my stables! Go find me the blackest, gothiest horse and start grooming it!"

The twins and Blendin realize that they can't argue with the newly crowned King Robbie.

For them, it looks like this is . . .

 THE END.

DRESS UP AS GUARDS TO ESCAPE

"**L**et's do like Chamillacles and hide in plain sight!" says Dipper, picking up a guard's uniform. There's a single chrono-blaster on the floor. Dipper sees Davy Time-Jones eye the weapon. Dipper scoops it up. "I'll hold on to this," he tells Davy. "I'm really starting to wonder if we can trust these guys," he mutters to Mabel.

They all quickly throw on guard uniforms over their inmate outfits and inspect their reflections in the shiny metal wall. They all look convincingly like time guards.

"I wish this was more slimming," says Blendin.

"A uniform just makes you feel so *powerful!*" says Mabel, slapping a nightstick into her palm.

Chamillacles mumbles something in Gleep-Glorp and points his scaly finger at the Guard Transport Station, a room filled with shiny tubes made for teleporting the guards back to Earth.

Suddenly, a battalion of backup guards rounds a corner and spots them!

For a long moment, the guards just stare at them.

"They're back that way! HUSTLE!" yells Mabel, pointing over her shoulder. "And give each other supportive back massages while you march!"

The guards straighten up and follow her orders.

"Yes, ma'am!" they shout, massage-marching their way down the hall.

"I'm really turning this place around!" says Mabel.

They approach the glass door to the Guard Transport Station.

Davy Time-Jones runs up to the door and mashes the security keypad to gain access. It doesn't work. He keeps entering the wrong code, and a red light flashes and a robotic voice says, "TOO MANY FAILED ENTRIES." A trapdoor opens in the floor.

Chamillacles falls in, shouting profanities in Gleep-Glorp until he's no longer in earshot.

The large chasm separates the gang from Davy Time-Jones. There's an electrical cord suspended from the ceiling that the twins and Blendin could use to swing across, but it's on Davy Time-Jones's side.

"Throw us the cord!" Dipper screams to him.

"We don't like holes or falling!" adds Mabel.

"No, throw me the blaster!" yells Davy Time-Jones. "I need to blast open this door!"

"Well, then help us swing across first!" yells Dipper.

"There's no time! Just throw me the blaster!"

"How do I know you won't double-cross us?"

"You don't!" yells Davy Time-Jones. "Now throw me the blaster!"

"More guards are coming!" yells Blendin. "We're running out of time!"

Dipper looks down at the weapon in his hands and then across the way at Davy Time-Jones.

What should he do? Can he trust Davy to throw him the cord? Or should Dipper just try to jump the chasm without it?

THROW THE WEAPON TO DAVY: GO TO PAGE 33

TRY TO JUMP OVER THE CHASM: GO TO PAGE 157

TRY TO ESCAPE WITH BLENDIN

"**I didn't trust Gleefuls in the past,** and I'm not trusting them in the future, either," Dipper whispers to Mabel. He turns to Glorglax Gleeful. "You know what, we took a chance and it didn't work out, so I just think we're gonna—NOW!"

Mabel throws a handful of sand at the sales-borg and they make a break for it.

Glorglax Gleeful screams. "AAAAH, my eyes! I need them to see rubes!"

The twins grab Blendin and run through the gate, out into a crowded marketplace.

"Ingenious!" exclaims Blendin. "How'd you know that Future-Sand is the sharpest, most painful substance on Earth?"

"Uh . . . we didn't," says Mabel. "He's okay, right?"

"Too late now! Let's split up to evade him," says Blendin. "Rendezvous under the giant statue of Time Baby in ten minutes!" Blendin separates from Dipper and Mabel.

But Glorglax has charged up his hover platform and is close behind.

"Hide!" screams Mabel.

The twins duck and dive through the crowded marketplace, past various time merchants selling all manner of time beads, time rugs, and time turtles, until they find themselves in a dead end!

"I've got you kids now!" Glorglax bellows. He speeds toward them.

Mabel spies a door. She pulls Dipper through and closes it.

The door locks behind them with a *THUD*.

"Phew, we're safe!" says Dipper.

"But where are we?" asks Mabel. Dipper whips out his flashlight and shines it into the dark hallway. There are rows of couches, flat-screen TVs, smartphones, and posters for movies Dipper and Mabel recognize.

"Everything is oddly familiar!" whispers Mabel.

"Yeah. What is this stuff?" asks Dipper. "Did we walk through a portal to our own time?"

They walk through a door and find themselves in a brightly lit empty middle school classroom. "This looks just like our school back in California!" says Mabel. "But why's it empty?"

Dipper tries to pick up an apple, but it's glued to the desk. "Mabel . . ." he says. "Something's off about this place. . . ."

Just then, Mabel spies a group of futuristic schoolchildren who are idly floating on hover boards and drinking hovering sodas.

"Hey, these kids will tell us what's going on!" she says. She walks up to talk to the kids and—

SMACK!

Mabel walks into an ultra-clear piece of glass.

All the kids turn to look at her and laugh, but she can't hear them.

"Dipper! We're trapped in some kind of glass box! It's just like the mimes warned us about!" Mabel screams.

Dipper looks on the wall and sees a large gold plaque. It reads:

— MUSEUM OF THE PAST —
MIDDLE SCHOOL, EARLY TWENTY-FIRST CENTURY

"Mabel . . . we're not in our own time!" he says. "We're trapped in a museum . . . of the past!"

Dipper and Mabel press their faces against the glass and see other glass boxes for different time periods: an office of workers at typewriters, with a plaque reading THE FIFTIES; a group of cavemen, with a plaque reading 100,000 BC; and a yawning guy wearing bell-bottoms under a disco ball, with a plaque reading THE WORST TIME.

"We have to get out! We have to get out!" says Mabel as she tries all the doors and windows.

But for anyone trapped inside the
Museum of the Past, it is surely . . .

 **THE END.**

THROW THE WEAPON TO DAVY

"**I** can't believe I'm about to trust a Time Pirate!" says Dipper as he tosses the weapon to Davy Time-Jones.

He catches it in his meaty hands, smirks, and points it at Dipper!

Dipper sighs. "It figures," he says, shielding Mabel and Blendin.

Davy Time-Jones fires and—

BOOOOOOOOOOSHHHHH!

—there's a flash of light.

The three clench their eyes shut and cringe. Then . . . the cry of a baby fills the air.

Dipper, Mabel, and Blendin open their eyes and spin

around. There on the ground behind them is a human baby in a pile of prison guard clothes.

"What happened?" asks Dipper.

"That guard was sneaking up on you, so I hit him with this reverse chrono-blaster," says Davy Time-Jones. "It reverses the age of any molecules!" He points it at a nearby bowl of fruit and shoots it.

Mabel looks inside. "Yup, they're all seeds now!" she says. "Neato!"

"Thanks, man," says Dipper.

Davy grins and tosses Dipper the cord. "Clock Kings for life."

Davy points the chrono-blaster at the glass door and fires, turning the glass into a pile of sand. He steps over it as the others swing across the chasm.

Inside the Guard Transport Station, Davy Time-Jones programs the teleporter. "I need to make sure it teleports us to a discreet location," he says. "We wouldn't wanna teleport into the middle of police headquarters! Hop on in and hold your breath. This is gonna be intense!"

"Man, this escape is so cool!" squeals Blendin, grabbing Davy's shoulders.

"Don't make this weird," says Davy.

Dipper, Mabel, and Blendin spot their laser blasters and clothing and snatch them up just as guards breach the door to the Guard Transport Station, opening fire.

The whole gang piles into the teleportation tube and Davy punches a button. There's a flash of light, and they all warp through quantum space. In another flash, with their lungs on the brink of bursting, they land on orange desert sand seemingly in the middle of nowhere.

Davy Time-Jones jumps up and down. "WOOOOOOO! We did it!" he says. "Can you believe it? We did it!" He gives Dipper a forceful high five that knocks Dipper to the ground.

They all bury their uniforms in the sand and prepare to go their separate ways.

Davy Time-Jones looks at the twins. "You guys really helped me out back there," he says. "It was a pleasure prison-breaking with you. I want to give you both honorary pirate hats." He hands each of them a pirate hat shoddily made from prison rags.

"I-is there one for me?" stammers Blendin.

Davy ignores him. "If there's anything else I can do for you kids, just let me know," he says.

Dipper and Mabel share a glance. "Actually, there is something," says Dipper. "We're looking for a key. . . ."

"A Time Key," says Mabel, unfurling Blendin's map and pointing to the illustration of the key. "Do you know anything about it?"

Davy Time-Jones smiles. "Of course I do!" he says. "The key you seek is—"

"FREEEZE!" yells Lolph, one of the Time Anomaly Enforcement Agents.

The gang spins around and they see that they are surrounded by cops.

"We've been had!" yells Davy Time-Jones.

One of the cops, Dundgren, points at Blendin. "Hey, look, it's that sweaty cop Blendin Blandin," he says. "He and the kids must be here working undercover! Come over here on this side of the law." He beckons Blendin and the twins to join him and the rest of the cops.

Blendin and Mabel start to walk toward them, but Dipper is frozen in place.

Davy Time-Jones stares at them all. "Dipper . . . you're . . . you're law enforcement?" he says. "You're not a Clock King after all?" He flips up his eye patch.

"Uhhhhh," says Dipper, looking from Davy Time-Jones to the cops. He looks into Davy Time-Jones's clock eye and watches a time tear fall from it. Dipper looks to Mabel and Blendin, who are urging him to join the police with them. Dipper bites his lip.

"Say it ain't so, Dipper! Help me thwart these cops!" says Davy Time-Jones.

The cops eye Dipper, crossing their arms.

"Well, whose side are you on, boy?" asks Lolph.

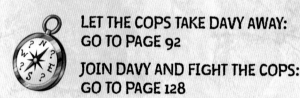

**LET THE COPS TAKE DAVY AWAY:
GO TO PAGE 92**

**JOIN DAVY AND FIGHT THE COPS:
GO TO PAGE 128**

COMMIT A GREAT TRAIN ROBBERY

"**W**hat should we do?" asks Blendin.

"Guys . . . do you hear that?" asks Mabel. "*Chugga-chugga* CHOO-CHOO! It's the sound of the great *train robbery train* coming into the station! Let's mount up some steeds, grab our six-shooters, and rob this iron horse! *Bang-bang!*"

"Hopefully we can find the Time Pirate who has the key!" agrees Dipper.

They high-five and head toward Loco Motive's Gun, Pony, and Bandana Store, next to the saloon.

"I dunno," says Blendin. "Train robberies aren't like what you see in the movies. Not to mention we'd be committing a crime on the turf of the legendary Calamity Brothers! Honestly, I think we'd be better off just impersonating passengers and sneaking aboard. That way, if we don't find the key, we can still slip away quietly without becoming fugitives for the rest of our time lives!"

"BOOOOOOOOOOOOOOOO," groans Mabel. "If people like you ran the world, we would have gone to the moon in hot air balloons instead of rockets."

"In the future, that's the only way we travel to the moon," says Blendin, confused.

"Let's put it to a vote!" says Mabel. She draws a line in the sand with a stick. "All in favor of doing it the fun way, stand on my side! All in favor of doing it the boring way, stand on Blendin's side."

Both Blendin and Mabel stare at Dipper.

Dipper looks at Loco Motive's, to his right. Across the street is Granny Huggins's Present-Timey Costume Shop.

Which plan should Dipper choose?

RIDE UP FROM THE OUTSIDE LIKE OUTLAWS: GO TO PAGE 164

SNEAK ABOARD THE TRAIN IN DISGUISE: GO TO PAGE 151

DOUBLE OR NOTHING

"**H**mmm. Let's take our chances!" says Dipper.

"Yeah!" says Mabel. "There's less oxygen in the air in the future and it's making me want to make dumb choices!" She rolls the probability square. "Come oooon, red!"

It lands on . . .

"BLUE! AGAIN!" yells Mabel.

Glorglax Gleeful bursts out laughing. "Well, well, well! I am just tickled pink by all of this," he says. "I woke up this morning and I thought to myself, I thought, *Glorglax, you are about three servants short of being able to polish all your droids all day every day for the rest of your life*, and then look. You guys walk in, and, well, it's just a miracle." He turns, digs through a closet, and pulls out a stack of linens. "Well, now here's some coarse beige cult-lookin' robes I expect you to wear while polishing them droids. And here's some soiled rags I expect y'all to do it with." He dumps the dirty linens in Dipper's, Mabel's, and Blendin's hands.

"Heh, heh, this, uh, sure is moving right along," says Mabel. "Are you sure you don't wanna try triple or nothing?"

The sales-borg claps his hands together and looks Mabel in the eyes. "Hmmmmmm. New rule: Servants don't talk! Now get to work!" he says, shoving the trio.

Dipper, Mabel, and Blendin settle in for a long day of polishing droids.

"Well, this is pretty much the worst thing that could have ever happened," says Dipper as he wipes sweat off his brow with a grease-smeared hand.

"Hey, look on the bright side," says Blendin. "We get a great view of the race! Yippee!"

"Did you actually just say 'yippee' sincerely?" asks Dipper.

"Not a lot of oxygen in the air, Dipper," says Blendin.

A speeder blasts by, covering them in dust.

They all cough.

Looks like for our heroes, this is . . .

 **THE END.**

TO BE VENGEFUL

"**N**O ONE SENDS MABEL TO HER DEATH AND GETS AWAY WITH IT!" Mabel roars. "We gotta go show this king what's up." She turns to the dragon. "Will you take us to him, Connerheart?"

"For you, anything!" says the dragon. "Climb upon me!"

The twins and Blendin scale his massive back.

"Hold on tightly!" With a flap of his enormous wings, he takes off. Soaring though the narrow cavern, he bursts forth into blinding daylight. The sunlight reflects off his red scales, making them gleam like wildfire. His yellow eyes flash, and his beating wings make a sound like a thunderstorm.

Passing villagers stop dead in their tracks (some from the plague) and stare.

Connerheart climbs higher and higher through the cloudless sky alongside a flock of birds. Dipper, Mabel, and Blendin watch the ground below shrink until it's just a patchwork quilt of farmland.

Mabel can't help squealing. "This is a delight!" she exclaims.

"I'm riding on a dragon!" says Dipper. "This adventure just got seriously legit!"

"I'm getting scale rash!" shrieks Blendin. "Does anyone wanna trade places?"

On the horizon, they spot the castle.

Connerheart dives toward it at full speed. He swoops in low over the buttressed walls and hovers outside the royal throne room.

Mabel addresses the king. "Mister King Man! Will you come out, please?" she yells.

Knights throw lances at the dragon, but they glance off his thick hide.

The king pokes his head through the window. "The, uh, king, is, uh, not here right now. Try back later," he says, trembling.

"I can see you, dum-dum!" says Mabel. She taps Connerheart on the head.

He spits out a fireball at the king, who squeals and ducks.

"Why'd you send us on a mission you hoped we wouldn't come back from?" asks Dipper. "You were never going to tell us about the Time Pirate and his Time Key, were you?"

"I was, I was!" cries the king.

"Don't lie to us!" says Mabel as she taps Connerheart again.

He sprays flames against the castle wall.

"Aaaaah!" screams the king. "That pirate person cameth here and gave me this key," he says, holding up the Time Key. It glints in the sunlight. "He swore he'd destroy me if I didn't keep it safe!"

"How can we believe you?" says Mabel. "This isn't another trick, is it?"

"Goodness, no!" says the king. "Look at how much I'm

shaking! I'm a coward whose every action is motivated by fear! Do you think I'd surround myself with strong knights in a castle and be a jerk to people if I wasn't deeply afraid of everything?"

"Hmmmm," says Mabel. She turns to her friends. "All right, guys, new plan. Connerheart, you stay here and make sure that the king is less of a jerk to the kingdom. King, you give us that key. Blendin, you take us to the time island. We've got a time treasure to collect."

The king tosses the Time Key to Mabel, who catches it.

"Well, what are we waiting for?" asks Dipper. "Let's get that time treasure!"

They bid farewell to Connerheart.

"Good luck!" the dragon says. "And thank you for helping me resolve my various deep-seeded emotional issues!"

Mabel finds Blendin's laser blasters stashed behind the king's throne and tosses them to Blendin. The trio huddles.

"Oooh, I'm so excited!" says Blendin. "My knees only shake this much when I think I'm going to be very rich very soon!" He motions to his jittering knees.

Mabel pokes one. It stops. She lets go and it starts shaking again. She does this several more times before Blendin knocks her hand away.

Blendin and the twins wrestle off their armor and Blendin produces the time tape from his jumpsuit. He holds the Time Key in his other hand.

Dipper and Mabel grab hold of the time tape together.

"Where we're going is very special," says Blendin. "It's not a time or a space but rather a place *between* time and space. Our lives flow on a river of time. And every choice we make is like traveling down a new unique branch of that river. If you could see the fourth dimension, you could see the entirety of human history sprawled out like a river delta. Infinite lives and parallel universes coexisting. And now we're about to step out of the river—onto a secret hidden island wedged between the currents of time!"

"Ooooh!" say Dipper and Mabel.

"I memorized that quote from a movie," says Blendin, beaming. "It was called *StellarCeption*, was forty-eight hours long, and was utterly incomprehensible. Very popular in time prison."

Blendin pulls out a measured length of time tape and lets go.

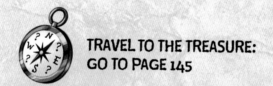

TRAVEL TO THE TREASURE:
GO TO PAGE 145

ROLL THE PROBABILITY SQUARE

"**Y**ou know what, Dipper? I'm feeling lucky!" says Mabel. She picks up the probability square and shakes it in her hand.

Blendin turns red. "You feel *lucky*?" he says. "The existence of luck was scientifically disproven in 20705! You're literally gambling with my life!"

Mabel looks at Dipper. "Blow on the cube?" she asks.

Dipper does, and Mabel rolls.

"Come ooooon, red!" cheer the twins.

The cube tumbles across the table, slowing down and rolling to a stop on . . .

"BLUE!" Mabel yells.

"Hoo-boy!" screams Glorglax Gleeful.

"AAAH, COME ON!" Blendin kicks a droid. It beeps and kicks him back.

"Now that is a tasty development," says Glorglax, wiping sweat from his brow. "But I can see y'all are rightfully upset. So how about this: you roll again, and if you win, you can keep your friend and buy the cruddy racer. But if I win, y'all two kids join your friend as my servants for life."

Dipper and Mabel turn to each other.

"Hmmmm . . . Dipper, should we risk our freedom to save Blendin's?" Mabel whispers.

They look at Blendin, who furiously nods.

"I dunno," whispers Dipper. "Couldn't we just, like, throw sand in his eyes and run away from the bet and forget the whole space race?"

"Oooh, that's an equally good idea!" whispers Mabel. "What do we do?"

Decisions, decisions.

DOUBLE OR NOTHING: GO TO PAGE 39

TRY TO ESCAPE WITH BLENDIN: GO TO PAGE 29

CONTINUE STALLING

"**U**h . . ." Dipper says.

The conductor grabs his baton. Then Blendin bursts in with his gentleman suitor. "How dare you harass my babies!"

The suitor sidles up next to him. "My name is P. B. Peckinbridge and I'm the owner of this here train and its cargo, and I demand you release my fair maiden's children!"

The conductor gawks. "They might be thieves!"

"They're children," says Mr. Peckinbridge. "They're just naturally curious!" The gentleman kneels before the twins. "Would you rapscallions like to see my treasure?"

Dipper's and Mabel's eyes widen and they nod.

"Well, here you go!" The gentleman procures a key from his overcoat and sticks it into the lock of the treasure safe.

The safe opens.

The twins' jaws drop as they see . . .

Grain. Lots of grain.

"Look at it, kids. Isn't it beautiful? It's grain! Beautiful grain. Life's only real treasure. Would you like to swim in it with me?" Mr. Peckinbridge asks.

Dipper and Mabel watch the grain pour onto the floor.

Mr. Peckinbridge dives into it. "Please, children," he says, "come swim in the grain with me."

The twins start walking away.

"Let's go, Blendin," Mabel says.

"Hey, do what you want! This guy is rich. I'm gonna stay here and milk this time pony!" says Blendin, stepping toward Mr. Peckinbridge swimming in the pile of grain.

The train jolts and Blendin's wig falls off.

Mr. Peckinbridge raises an eyebrow. "Blendinella! You— you lied to me!"

Blendin freezes.

Mr. Peckinbridge sits up and hangs his head. "Please," he says, holding out a hand, "just . . . go."

The twins and Blendin leave the train and wander back to town, taking off their cumbersome costumes as they go.

"Well, that was clearly the wrong choice!" says Mabel. "But we've got two options left—confront the outlaws or inspect the mine!"

"What about lying down in a fetal position and giving up forever?" asks Blendin hopefully.

"That's not an option!" says Mabel.

EMBARK ON A MINING ADVENTURE: GO TO PAGE 255

CONFRONT THE OUTLAWS IN THE SALOON: GO TO PAGE 237

FLY INTO THE ASTEROID FIELD

"**I** think this is one of those situations best handled by running away," says Mabel. She points their spaceship toward the asteroid field and away from the giant spaceship. She jams the throttle to the floor and their spacecraft gains speed. The gang watches as the large ship slows behind them. They all jump up and down and cheer.

General Crustaceous Lob-Star appears again on the communication screen. "We can wait, you know. We can wait forever—" The screen goes haywire with electrical static. The general disappears. His image is replaced by an episode of *Shimmery Twinkleheart*, a 1980s kids' cartoon show in which a plump star in short-shorts teaches after-school lessons.

"*Shimmery Twinkleheart*? I haven't seen this in years! What's it doing on here? In space? In the future?" asks Mabel.

Dipper looks out the window. "Whoa, these aren't asteroids at all," he says. "This is a debris field! These are all old satellites!" He gestures toward the seemingly endless field of space junk.

Broken Soviet, cable TV, and spy satellites all bleep uselessly.

"The old signals of TV and radio shows must be bouncing around out here infinitely," says Dipper. "That's why we can pick it up!"

"That's so cool! We should watch an episode!" says Mabel.

"*Gleep glorp glorp!*" says Chamillacles.

"Yeah, I wanna see what the star in short-shorts has to teach me about life!" says Davy Time-Jones. "Also, maybe it'll teach me how to read."

Dipper sits down and watches an episode with the rest of them.

Soon one episode turns into two.

Two turns into an entire season.

They find old episodes of *Duck-tective, Tiger Fist, Ghost Harassers,* and *The Duchess Approves,* and start watching them.

As it turns out, the prison guard ships never tire of waiting for them.

But there are probably worse fates than being forced to watch TV forever. Actually, on second thought, there aren't. For our heroes, it looks like . . .

 **THE END.**

LET THE WIZARD GO

"**D**ipper, remember when Mom and Dad made you take piano lessons and you hated it because you really just wanted to play the tuba?" asks Mabel.

"Uh, n-no," stammers Dipper, eyes darting back and forth as he clears his throat.

"This is just like that!" she says. "We can't force this wizard—what's your name again?"

"Magnarfus the Magnificent," says the wizard.

"Whatever," says Mabel. "We can't force Muffin-Pants the Mysterious to be something he's not. He's a caged bird. He longs to fly free!"

"You realize I'm an adult and can make my own decisions, right?" says Magnarfus.

"Well, I guess we better go back to the king and tell him we failed," says Blendin.

"Oh, no, no, no! You can't go back to the king without me," says the wizard. "He'll throw you in the dungeon for the rest of your lives!"

"But life is so long! And I was just starting to hit my stride," says Dipper.

"And now we'll never find the Time Pirates' Treasure!" adds Mabel.

"Here, come with me and help me escape," says

the wizard. "I can't give you this so-called Time Pirates' Treasure, but I'll make it worth your while!"

"A vague promise from an unreliable wizard? Count me *in*!" says Mabel.

The wizard empties a cabinet full of potions into a bag and opens a door at the back of the room.

"This way will lead us out of the castle," he says. The wizard takes a deep breath and looks around at his workshop. His desk, his chair. His cage filled with live toads. "So many memories," he sighs. "Well, time to blow up this place for the insurance money." He takes a potion from his bag, pulls the cork from the bottle with his teeth, and rolls it into the chamber like a hand grenade. "RUN!" he yells as he sprints away from the workshop.

The whole gang is booking it down the passageway and up a winding staircase when—

BOOM!

The workshop explodes behind them.

There's a brilliant flash of light, and a wall of rainbow flames chases them.

They run as fast as they can up the stairs and leap out a castle window into the sky as a fireball shoots out behind them. They fall and land in a shallow moat of brackish water.

"Ow, I think I hurt my everything," says Mabel.

"Me too," says Dipper.

"I'm all right. But my jumpsuit is filled with frogs now,"

says Blendin as he unzips his jumpsuit, letting them spill out.

The gang swims to the shore.

The wizard coughs and waves his wand. *"Everybodius Dryus!"* he says, and the gang immediately dries off. Mabel's hair also now has a perm.

"Oooh, I am loving this," she says.

"Thank you so much for helping me escape," says the wizard. "I know you've come here in search of something, and that helping me has now made that dream impossible. So I'd like to offer you a reward as just compensation."

"Ooooh, yes!" says Blendin. "Daddy wants some time treats!"

"I have here two potions," says the wizard. "One will give you the power to turn anything to gold. The other will give you eternal youth. Either can be yours. Choose wisely."

The group huddles together.

"Which one do we pick?" asks Dipper.

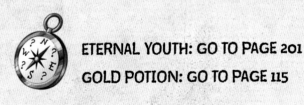

ETERNAL YOUTH: GO TO PAGE 201

GOLD POTION: GO TO PAGE 115

GO THE OTHER WAY

"**Ohhhh, darn my luck, I pulled a muscle!**" says Dipper unconvincingly. He looks at Jugsley, who squints at him. "We should probably go this other way. . . . It looks a little easier to walk."

Jugsley gets a vacant look in his eyes and then cackles.

Dipper, Mabel, and Blendin back away, trembling.

"It's funny you should say that!" says Jugsley. "I was trying real hard to lead you one way so's I could kill ya and steal your stuff. But I just realized, it doesn't matter which way you go. I'm still gonna kill ya!" He lets out a devious laugh and pulls a rusty pickax from the wall.

The friends look at each other, and then they make a run for it.

Jugsley races after them.

They dash down the path without looking back.

"Where are we going?" shouts Mabel.

"I don't know!" shouts Dipper. "Away from him!"

They round a corner into what looks like a dead end. Behind them, they hear the echo of the pickax scraping along the granite floors.

"End of the line, little nuggets," says Jugsley.

To the left of the group is an abandoned mine cart on tracks leading down a dark tunnel. To their right is a pile of dynamite connected to a detonator.

"Guys, we have two choices," says Dipper. "Either we escape by taking a dangerous mine-cart ride into the dark abyss or blow up the tunnel behind us and risk trapping ourselves."

"Isn't there a third option? Like diplomacy?" asks Mabel.

"No!" says the prospector, rounding the bend and starting to close the distance between them.

"Sorry, guys, we gotta pick our poison," says Dipper.

Mabel bites her lip. "Dipper, what do we do?"

USE DYNAMITE TO CAVE IN THE PATH: GO TO PAGE 85

ESCAPE IN THE MINE CART: GO TO PAGE 184

FLY PAST THE GIANT SHIP

"As captain of this ship,** I've decided that the best course of action is to sail straight for that gigantic obstacle head-on!" says Mabel. "I'm sure that's never backfired at any point in history!" She punches some buttons, and their spaceship somersaults and zips toward the enormous ship looming ahead of them.

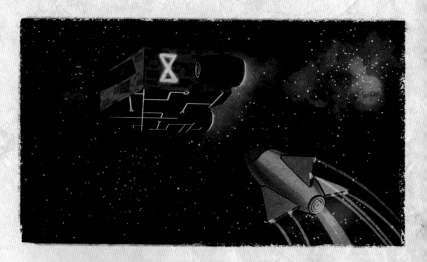

"You're crazy, kid! I love it!" yells Davy Time-Jones.

Blendin gulps, becoming somehow even paler than normal.

On the ship's communication screen, they see General Crustaceous Lob-Star. "They're coming back at us! What can we do?" he screams at his crew. "We're dead if they attack the bridge with their torpedoes!" He stops and looks at the camera. "Wait, is my feed turned on? Ah, son of a—" The screen goes black.

"Did you guys hear that?" asks Dipper. "If we shoot our torpedoes at the bridge, we can take out the whole ship!"

"Great plan," says Blendin. "Except we don't actually *have* any torpedoes. Best we could do is jettison our fuel tanks and hope they strike. But that's pretty risky!"

"Also, I think that lobster general is adorable and I don't wanna mess up him or his pretty ship," says Mabel. "What else could we do?"

Chamillacles warbles and then pulls up a 3-D schematic of the enemy ship. He points a scaly finger at an exhaust port on the front.

Davy Time-Jones smiles. "If we enter that exhaust port," he says, "then we can just fly out the other side! Assuming we can make the incredibly dangerous flight!"

Mabel scrunches up her face.

Both these options seem super dangerous.
Which should Mabel choose?

TAKE OUT THE BRIDGE: GO TO PAGE 279

FLY THROUGH THE SHIP: GO TO PAGE 234

TAKE THE WIZARD TO THE KING

"**P**lease, pretty please, please, please!" begs the wizard. "I'll do anything to—"

"*SILENCIUS, WIZARDIUS!*" yells Mabel.

The wizard continues flapping his lips, but he no longer has a voice.

"Whoa, what are the odds that would work?" says Mabel, beaming. "I just made that up! I guess wizard spells are stupidly easy to guess!"

"Awesome!" says Dipper.

"Let's get this guy to the king!" says Mabel. She starts poking the wizard with his own wand as Blendin leads the way out of the workshop.

✦ ✦✦ ✦

In the royal throne room, the gang presents the wizard to the king.

"Here, Your Royal Highness, is the missing wizard!" says Dipper.

"Oh, goodie, goodie!" says the king. "Guards, take him to the tower! There's a company birthday party happening right now! Make sure he signs the card for everyone!"

"NOOOO!" screams the wizard as they drag him away.

"Thank you, children. Your services are no longer needed," the king says with a clap, inviting the guards to remove the twins and Blendin from his presence.

"Whoa, whoa, hold on," says Dipper, pushing them away. "We only did this because you promised us you'd tell us about the pirate. You owe us, man."

"What?" says the king. "I remember none of this! Surely you must be confused. Guards!"

His guards point the sharp ends of their pikes directly at Dipper, Mabel, and Blendin.

"But, of course, you have done my kingdom a great service," says the king. "Maybe if you were to help with one of my other tasks, I could find it appropriate to help you out."

"*What?*" says Mabel. "If you didn't help us the first time, then why should we trust you?"

"Because you have no other choice!" says the king. "My guards have pointy weapons, remember?"

Dipper and Mabel grumble.

"Ugh, he's got us there," says Dipper.

"So, what are you saying we do, Dipper?" asks Mabel.

"Obviously, we either need to fight that dragon or that knight. Preferably whichever one is less work."

The twins and Blendin think over what to do.

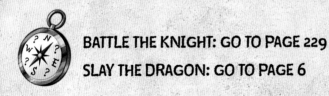

BATTLE THE KNIGHT: GO TO PAGE 229
SLAY THE DRAGON: GO TO PAGE 6

ACCEPT DOS HUNTHOU AS THEIR OWN

"**D**ipper, we have no choice but to take him in as our own," says Mabel. "I mean, look at him, he needs us!" Mabel points at Dos Hunthou, who is rummaging through trash and sniffing the ground like a dog.

"Ugh, you're right," says Dipper. "Let's just drop him off with Grunkle Stan and get on with getting this treasure!"

Dipper and Mabel shake off their racer suits and join Blendin, who pulls the time tape and sends them all back to Gravity Falls.

Outside the Mystery Shack, Soos is raking the lawn.

"Hey, Soos!" says Mabel.

"Oh, man! 'Sup, dudes? Who's this terrifying shirtless guy?" Soos points at Dos Hunthou.

"Long story, but we went to the future and won this guy in a race," says Dipper. "He's kind of like our manservant now. Can you look after him while we go and get the Time Pirates' Treasure?"

"Yeah, totally, dudes!" says Soos. "What should I do with him?"

Mabel shrugs. "I dunno," she says. "Feed him, I guess. And maybe put him to work if you need it."

Soos squints, rubs his chin, and then smiles. "I will teach you my ways," he says to Dos Hunthou. "Prepare to learn eighty-seven different types of high five."

Dos Hunthou gives Soos a slight smile and nods.

Dipper holds up the Time Key. "All right, you guys!" he says, turning to Mabel and Blendin. "We have the Time Key! Now let's get to that treasure!"

"Oooh, I'm so excited!" says Blendin. "My knees only shake this much when I'm near treasure!" He motions to his jittering knees.

Mabel pokes one. It stops. She lets go and it starts shaking again. She does this several more times before Blendin knocks her hand away.

Blendin lifts his time tape in one hand and takes the Time Key from Dipper in the other.

The twins grab hold of the time tape together.

"Where we're going is very special," says Blendin. "It's not a time or a space but rather a place *between* time and space. Our lives flow on a river of time. And every choice we make is like traveling down a new, unique branch of that river. If you could see the fourth dimension, you could see the entirety of human history sprawled out like a river delta. Infinite lives and parallel universes coexisting. And now we're about to step out of the river—onto a secret hidden island wedged between the currents of time!"

"Oooh!" say Dipper and Mabel.

"I memorized that quote from a movie," says Blendin, beaming. "It was called *StellarCeption*, was forty-eight hours long, and was utterly incomprehensible. Very popular in time prison."

Blendin pulls out a measured length of time tape and lets go.

TRAVEL TO THE TREASURE: GO TO PAGE 145

PERFORM A HIGH-SPEED BOARDING

"**Forget it!**" **yells Mabel.** "We're going in! Yah! Black-Spirit-Beauty-Biscuit, away!" She urges her horse across the dusty plain, passing cacti and saw grass, and gallops up parallel to a railcar.

Dipper and Blendin fall in behind her.

She makes a grasp for the railing and grabs hold of it.

"How is she so good at this?" asks Blendin, panting.

"Mabel went through a 'country phase' in fifth grade," says Dipper. "Just be glad she doesn't say 'y'all' anymore."

"Wow, I think we might actually pull this off!" says Blendin. "Nothing can stop us now! Yee-haw-AAUGH!"

As Blendin tries to yell like a cowboy, he slips and falls off his horse and tumbles to the ground. "HELP! MAN DOWN!" he shrieks as he rolls like a tumbleweed.

Dipper and Mabel sigh and circle back.

"Blendin, are you okay?" asks Mabel.

"Y-y-y-y-y-yeah, I'm good, I think," stammers Blendin. "I experience head injuries about three times a day, so I got this."

"Well, there goes our chance of ever getting on that train," says Dipper as he watches it speed off into the distance.

"Awww, it's okay," says Mabel.

"Hey, what's that sound?" asks Dipper.

Pebbles shake at their feet.

"Huh, it sounds like rumbling. Maybe it's the train! Maybe they decided to come back and let us rob them after all!" says Mabel.

"No, it's not coming from the tracks. . . . It's coming from . . . behind us?" says Dipper. He wheels his horse around to see . . . hundreds of lawmen racing across the plain toward them.

"Freeze, you fiendish outlaws! Put your hands up!" screams the sheriff.

"Ah, nuts, it's the fuzz!" yells Blendin.

"What do we do, what do we do?" asks Mabel.

"Well, we either surrender peacefully or make a run for it," answers Dipper.

"I want a third option!" says Blendin.

"It doesn't work that way!" screams Mabel. "IT NEVER WORKS THAT WAY!"

MAKE A RUN FOR IT: GO TO PAGE 170

SURRENDER: GO TO PAGE 281

DECLINE BLENDIN'S OFFER

Mabel shrugs. "Eh," she says.

"Sorry, man, I think we're gonna sit this one out," says Dipper. "I'd love to help, but it's like . . . Time Pirates . . . and carrying stuff."

"Yeah, but don't get discouraged! You're a shining star!" says Mabel. She peels a glimmering star from her sticker book and affixes it to Blendin's chest. "Never give up on your dreams," she whispers in his ear.

"Oh, all right," says Blendin, frowning. "Just remember, you won't be getting any of this sweet, sweet time treasure!"

The twins shrug and walk away.

"You know, Dipper, I feel like we made a great choice," says Mabel.

"Yeah, Mabel, I agree!" says Dipper. "Now let's forget all about that treasure."

They go back to the Mystery Shack and turn on the TV. There's a marathon of documentaries about treasure hunts running on the Used to Be About History Channel. Frowning, Mabel changes the channel and sees a documentary called *Wrong Choices*.

"There are people who make terrible choices," says the host, "and the long-lasting psychological effects of regret follow these people forever!"

"Ummm . . . Mabel, do you think the universe is trying to tell us something?" asks Dipper.

Mabel scratches her chin. "Like that maybe we missed the adventure of a lifetime?"

"Don't worry, Mabel, this is Gravity Falls! I'm sure another adventure will come our way today," says Dipper.

The twins sit in silence for an hour.

A fly lands on Dipper's hand.

"Oooh, a fly! Is it a paranormal fly?" asks Mabel.

"No, regular fly," says Dipper.

Mabel coughs.

Nice choice, reader! You've already
brought our adventure to . . .

 **THE END.**

DISTRACT THE OUTLAWS AND RUN

Dipper pulls out his flashlight and shines it in Wild Eyes Joe's face.

Wild Eyes Joe releases Dipper's shoulder, covers his eyes, and screams. "There's a miniature sun in his hands!" he shouts. "He's a witch!"

"Everyone, now!" yells Dipper. "Distract them with our future stuff!"

Mabel grabs a handful of glitter and blows it at the outlaws.

"AAAH! Witch powder!" screams one outlaw.

The others try to brush the glitter off themselves, but it's stuck to their dusters.

Blendin reaches in his pockets and finds a laminated

ID. He shakes it at the outlaws. They back away from him and scream, shielding their faces.

"It's smooth like glass! But it bends like a Turkish dancer!" one screams before leaping face-first out a plate-glass window.

"Get your devil toys away from us, witches!" yells Wild Eyes Joe.

Blendin and the twins back toward the door.

Mabel points at the minions and says, "Stay back! Stay back or we'll use our powers to turn you into muffins! Or force you to kiss each other!"

The outlaws cringe.

"On the count of three, we're gonna make a run for it," whispers Dipper.

Mabel and Blendin nod.

"Okay," says Dipper. "One . . . two . . . thr—"

"HOLD IT RIGHT THERE!" says someone with a booming voice.

Dipper, Mabel, and Blendin whirl around.

Shopkeeper Sprott has gathered a witch-hunting posse. "Now, I knew y'all were witches since I first laid eyes on you," he says, "so I gathered up this here huntin' squad to send you back to Lucifer's claws, where y'all belong." He laughs. "Let's burn 'em up, boys."

The glaring townsfolk take hold of the twins and Blendin and drag them toward the town square. They set them up on a pyre and stack kindling beneath.

Dipper looks at Blendin. "Well, now we're being burned at the stake. Really awesome adventure, Blendin. Five stars."

Blendin stammers, "I-I'm sorry, I guess I got carried away looking for this treasure. Should we just go home instead?"

"Absolutely," say the twins in unison.

Blendin pulls the time tape and they disappear in an electric-blue flash. Shopkeeper Sprott stands quietly for a moment and shrugs. "Welp, I reckon we've all been touched by the hand of the devil himself," he says.

The mob turns his way.

✦ ✦✦ ✦

The twins and Blendin arrive back in Gravity Falls. They pat down the remaining sparks in their clothes, and Dipper and Mabel say good-bye to Blendin. On their walk home, they pass by Farmer Sprott, who's raising a scarecrow.

Dipper pauses. "Hey, can I ask you why you hate witches so much?"

"Why, yes, you can," Farmer Sprott says. "I reckon it's 'cause my great-great-great-great-grandpappy way out west was burnt alive for letting a group o' witches escape, and my family has sworn to avenge him going on seven generations now!"

"Huh," says Mabel. She looks at Dipper. "Do you think we should feel bad?"

Dipper shrugs. "Well, if the Farmer Sprott we knew

already hated witches, that means that this chain of events we just experienced was bound to happen regardless, and had happened before we even experienced it."

"And therefore, free will is an illusion!" says Mabel. "Yay!"

The twins silently stare into the distance for a minute.

"Let's never discuss time travel again," says Dipper.

"Deal," says Mabel.

 THE END

BROOM SERVICE

"**H**e ordered *broom* service!" yells Blendin.

"WHAT? Wizards don't use brooms! You're thinking of witches! I'm offended! The correct answer was he *wandered* around!" says the wizard, sneering. He claps his hands and the room stops filling with cola. It starts draining.

"Wait," says Dipper, "you're not going to drown us?"

"Oh, heavens, no, I would never do such a thing. People aren't fun at all when they're dead. Besides, you're more valuable to me alive. Since you're apparently terrible at guessing riddles, you'll be the perfect test audience for me to try out a thousand more riddles I was working on."

"We were kind of hoping to leave," says Mabel.

"Hey, here's a riddle! Who's now trapped in here for all eternity?" asks the wizard.

"N-not us?" says Blendin.

"WRONG AGAIN!" screams the wizard, grinning. "Okay, here's a good one. What did the wizard say to the ostrich while they were potion shopping? Hint: the answer is long and obscure!"

Everyone groans in unison.

For our heroes, it looks like . . .

 THE END.

DIPPER TALKS

Dipper shrugs and smiles. "I'm clearly on fire today!" he says. "I got this." He coughs and clears his throat. "*Attention*, passengers of the *Calamity Limited*! My name's Dead-Eye Dipper Pines, and we're here to—"

A breeze blows across the open plain, filling Dipper's nose with pollen and causing him to—

"*Achoo!*"

—sneeze like a kitten.

All the train passengers giggle.

"Ignore that! Everyone ignore that! Forget that!" says Dipper. He brandishes the laser blaster. "LIKE I SAID, turn over your treasure or—*achoo!*" Dipper sneezes again.

Everyone giggles again.

"By Jove, he sneezes like a kitten!" exclaims a passenger with a handlebar mustache.

"That's the most adorable thing I've ever seen!" says a passenger in a bonnet and petticoat.

"Why, these bandits aren't threatening at all! They're delightful!" says yet another passenger. "Here, someone give this adorable little boy a frilly handkerchief and let's carry on our way!"

Everyone on the train nods.

A surly male passenger dressed in black produces a kerchief, saunters up, and gives it to Dipper.

Dipper looks at the man, who seems oddly familiar as he walks away, spurs clinking with each step.

"Take care of yourself now, y'hear?" the man says as all the passengers return to their seats.

At the front of the train, the conductor yells, "Rocks are cleared. Back on our way!"

The train lurches forward, with all the passengers on board laughing about what just happened and doing kitten-sneeze impressions.

"What a waste of time," says Dipper, looking at the handkerchief he was just handed. His jaw drops. "Or was it? I knew that guy looked familiar! Look at the initials on this handkerchief! W. E.! Wyatt Earp!"

"The heartthrob pop star?" asks Mabel, her eyes shining.

"No!" says Dipper. "The most famous lawman of all

time, and he just gave me his handkerchief! Do you know how valuable this is? We could probably sell this in the future and make a fortune!"

"Or take it to the way, *way* future and use Wyatt Earp's DNA to make an army of clones!" says Mabel. "You guys can do that, right?"

"But what about the Time Pirates' Treasure?" asks Blendin.

"Honestly, I'm kind of over it," says Dipper.

"Me too," says Mabel. "Wanna cash out this kerchief and go play video games?"

"Do I ever!" says Dipper.

The twins take Blendin's time tape and return to the present.

They walk into the Mystery Shack and Stan is there to greet them.

"Grunkle Stan, you'll never guess what we found!" says Dipper, waving the kerchief at him.

"Oh, good! Just what I needed!" says Stan, taking the hanky and sneezing up, down, and all around into it. He hands it back to Dipper. "Now, what were you saying?"

Dipper sighs. "Never mind," he says, throwing the hanky in the trash.

"Hey, I know what'll cheer you up!" says Grunkle Stan. "Check out this new attraction I got. It's a penny arcade machine from the Old West! It depicts a real historical train robbery!"

Grunkle Stan gestures to an ancient rusty brass machine and plunks in a penny. A tiny curtain opens, revealing a model train filled with tiny toy passengers. A cowboy puppet pops up with a word bubble reading ACHOO! The model passengers pop up on springs. A caption rises on a stick: YONDER FOOL SNEEZES AS WOULD A KITTEN! WHAT A JACKANAPES!

Mabel can't help laughing.

"I'm destroying this machine," says Dipper.

 **THE END**

REFUSE TO MARRY THE KING'S DAUGHTER

"**E**hhh, I'm good, man," says Dipper. "It's nothing personal. I just don't know you that well, and marriage is kind of a big deal, and I'm only twelve and I have this really specific plan about meeting my future wife in college and being friends with her for a long time before she realizes we're perfect for each other. I'm pretty sure her name will be Jessica."

The king stares, mouth agape.

"What he's saying is, marriage would just be like . . . whaaaaa?" explains Mabel.

The king's expression hardens. "So, if I am to understand you correctly," he says, "you refuse to marry my daughter?"

"Yeah, pretty much. Sorry, dude," says Dipper.

"Then so be it! Guards!" yells the king. "Take him to the stable!"

"What? Why?" asks Dipper.

"The winner of the joust is required by *law* to marry someone! So if you don't marry my daughter, then I'll marry you off to my prize donkey!" bellows the king.

The guards grab Dipper, Mabel, and Blendin by their arms and start to drag them away.

"Wait! No! I'll just marry your daughter!" yells Dipper.

"Too little too late," says the king as he turns his back on Dipper.

✦ ✦✦ ✦

The stable is a filthy rectangular room buried deep beneath the castle. Rats scurry across its hay-covered floor. The guards lead Dipper down the hall to a small cobblestone-floored room where, awaiting him, is his bride-to-be: a large braying donkey.

"This is Ms. Gobblesnout," says the knight. "She'll be your wife."

"Question," says Mabel. "Does Ms. Gobblesnout have a maid of honor and can I be her maid of honor?"

"I don't see why not," says the knight.

Mabel pumps her fist. "Yesssss!"

Dipper glares at Mabel.

"What? This is happening, we might as well try to enjoy it!" she says.

And so, with Blendin as his best man and Mabel as the maid of honor, Dipper marries Ms. Gobblesnout. They all spend the rest of their lives in a barn feeding her hay.

And while Dipper and Ms. Gobblesnout never share what they consider to be "true love" or affection, they do have a stable, consistent marriage based on trust and open communication.

 **THE END**

USE DYNAMITE TO CAVE IN THE PATH

"**T**he detonator!" shouts Dipper.

Mabel takes a deep breath and pushes down the plunger.

BOOM!

There's a tremendous explosion and rocks fall around them in a calamitous debris slide.

Mabel, Dipper, and Blendin hit the ground and cover their heads.

As the rocks settle, they look up.

"We've done it!" says Dipper. "The path is sealed!"

"Yay!" says Mabel. "We blocked out that creepy prospector!"

"I heard that," says Jugsley from the other side of the debris. "Dagnabbit! Flibberjibbet!"

Blendin and the twins high-five.

"Take that, you bearded lunatic!" says Dipper.

"Um, Dipper," says Mabel. "The ground hasn't stopped shaking."

She, Dipper, and Blendin pause.

The ground is trembling.

"Did we cause an earthquake or something?" asks Dipper.

"Oh, no!" shouts Blendin. "Everyone hold on to something!"

The floor cracks and black liquid shoots out like a geyser. It hits the ceiling above and breaks a hole through it.

"Hooray! We've struck dirty water!" exclaims Mabel.

"It's *oil*, Mabel!" says Dipper, grinning. "And it just created a way out!"

They climb to the surface and survey their claim.

"Do you realize what this means?" yells Blendin. "We're oil rich! The best kind of rich! We don't need the treasure anymore! And I can wear a cowboy hat and call myself something like Big Hoss and people will be too intimidated to make fun of me!"

The twins cheer.

✦ ✦✦ ✦

A couple of hours later, Blendin and the twins have worked out an arrangement: Blendin will stay in the past to monitor the oil-drilling operations and will put a portion of the money aside for Dipper and Mabel. He'll bury it in the ground, and when they get to the future, they can dig up their profits. The twins think it's a great idea and say good-bye to Blendin. Dipper pulls the time tape, and they flash back to the future, ready to claim their reward. But something seems amiss. Gravity Falls doesn't look exactly like Gravity Falls anymore. The sky has a dark-red apocalyptic color. There are bars on every window and graffiti on every wall. It looks like a war-torn nightmare. Dipper and Mabel are uneasy.

"Dipper, what happened to our home?" asks Mabel.

They stumble backward and discover that the statue of Nathaniel Northwest has been replaced with one of Toby Determined.

Dipper and Mabel gasp.

"Mabel, read the statue's inscription," says Dipper, stepping forward.

— IN HONOR OF —

HE WHO FOUND BILLIONS IN GOLD BURIED

IN THE WOODS AND USED IT TO BUY MACHINES

OF TERROR THAT KEEP US IN OUR LOWLY PLACES:

TOBY DETERMINED, SUPREME RULER OF ALL GRAVITY FALLS.

OBEY HIM OR HA-CHA-CHA.

"This is horrible!" says Mabel.

"It's okay, we can undo this Toby-geddon!" says Dipper. He pulls out the time tape but is completely horrorstruck as he discovers that oil has gotten in its circuits and it's broken. The present is now permanent.

Looks like for them, this reality is . . .

 **THE END.**

GO THROUGH WITH THE MARRIAGE

"**M**abel, I have to do this," says Dipper.

"But what about the treasure?" asks Mabel.

"Uh, I dunno. Isn't love the greatest treasure of all or something?" asks Dipper.

"Awww, you're such a dork," says Mabel, ruffling his hair. "Maybe you *should* get married while you have the chance!"

At a small private ceremony, beneath grapevines in a garden, Dipper marries Wendinella.

He experiences his first kiss, and it's everything he's ever dreamed of. He gazes into Wendinella's eyes, and she gazes back. Dipper knows he's made the right choice.

He says good-bye to Mabel and Blendin and encourages them to visit often. He gives them a note to pass along to Stan and his parents, explaining what happened.

Dipper and Wendinella travel to their new castle in their new kingdom. It's a stately lot in the mountains, where pristine towers fly banners emblazoned with the Pines family crest.

"What a perfect place to spend the rest of our lives together," says Dipper.

"Yes, indeed," says Wendinella. "For only death will tear us apart." She coughs.

"Whoa, what's with the cough?" asks Dipper.

"'Tis nothing, my man," says Wendinella. She coughs again. "Probably just a mild plague. Everyone gets these at one point or another."

Dipper starts to sweat. He knows his bad luck well enough to know that this is one of those situations where, in an ironic twist, Wendinella will probably die and leave him broken and alone, regretting his choice.

But she doesn't.

In fact, Dipper and Wendinella go on to lead very happy lives together. They rule the kingdom with grace and generosity but still make serfs form human pyramids and wear silly tunics every Thursday. It's a good compromise. Sometimes they go around solving strange medieval mysteries together. Wendinella also encourages Dipper to use his knowledge of the future to write vague, terrifying prophecies about the twentieth century, just to mess with people. These writings are published under the pseudonym Nostradamus.

"I can't believe this actually worked out," says Dipper. "I sure pity any parallel universe version of me that didn't go through with this!"

They laugh, and they shockingly live happily ever after.

Aw, how sweet. It would've been sweeter with some Time Pirates' Treasure, though.

 THE END

LET THE COPS TAKE DAVY AWAY

Dipper looks back into Davy Time-Jones's watery clock eye. He looks at the Time Anomaly Enforcement Agents, hangs his head, and says, "We're . . . we're on your side."

Dundgren smirks. "Clock him up, boys," he says, and the two officers holding Davy Time-Jones start to drag him away.

Davy Time-Jones digs his heels into the ground and tries to wrest himself free. "You betrayed me!" he shouts at Dipper. "I thought we were Clock Kings for life!"

Dipper looks down at his shoes. He thinks about all the fun times they had together: throwing food, turning a prison guard into a baby, crossing that chasm. . . .

Davy Time-Jones breaks free of the guards and charges Dipper. He grabs the pirate hat from Dipper's head, throws it on the ground, and spits on it.

The officers grab him again and drag him away toward a space ship that makes a swift landing and opens its door.

"YOU BETRAYED ME, DIPPER PINES!" Davy Time-Jones bellows. "AND IT WILL HAUNT YOU TO YOUR DYING DAY!" He's taken into the ship and flown away.

A tumbleweed rolls by in the strange arid space desert.

"Well, time to keep moving!" says Mabel with a smile.

Dipper picks up his pirate hat. The trio starts to walk away. Suddenly the ship returns, lands before them, and Lolph and Dundgren leap out.

"Hold it right there," says Lolph. "We checked our system, and it turns out you're not an undercover time cop, Blendin! You're coming with us!" He slaps time cuffs on Blendin's wrists and drags him away.

"And you kids are going home," says Dundgren. He whisks them back to the present.

✦ ✦✦ ✦

Back at the Mystery Shack, things return to normal. Stan makes breakfast for the twins, Mabel bedazzles her pirate hat and develops new crushes, and Dipper tells Soos all about their non-canon time adventure.

But every night, Dipper stares at his soiled pirate hat, truly haunted by guilt . . . forever.

 THE END

FIGHT THE TIME PIRATES

Time Beard and his crew move to seize Blendin.

"Blendin may be dumb—" says Mabel.

"Hey!" says Blendin.

"—and he may be a terrible time traveler—" says Mabel.

"The worst!" says Dipper.

"Aw, come on!" says Blendin.

"—but he's our *friend*, and we're gonna stand by him!" Mabel finishes. She draws a rusty cutlass from the sand.

Dipper follows suit.

"Yarrrrrrghh, clock your time muskets!" says Time Beard.

His crew shoves watches and clock parts into front-loading flintlock pistols.

With a time-shaking thud, the *T. rex* leaps off the ship and into the sand with one of the pirates on its back. The dinosaur kicks its feet in the sand menacingly.

"If it's a time battle ye want, it's a time battle ye'll get!" says Time Beard. "Attack!"

His crew charges Blendin and the twins.

The gang charges back.

Dipper ducks under a volley of clock fire, leaps up, and locks cutlasses with a Time Pirate, then kicks the pirate's legs out from under him.

Mabel dashes across the sand toward a particularly burly Time Pirate.

He swings his sword at her, but Mabel ducks under his legs, scales his back, and pulls his hat over his eyes.

Blendin fires both of the laser blasters he brought along. Portals to other times open everywhere. A shark leaps out of one, grabs a Time Pirate, and pulls him through the portal.

"ENOUGH! Attack with the dinosaur!" says Time Beard.

The Time Pirate riding the *T. rex* charges toward Blendin, knocking Time Pirates out of the way. The dinosaur head-butts Blendin and knocks him onto the sand before reeling back to deliver a final blow.

Dipper sees this over his shoulder. He turns back to grab his cutlass but finds himself face to face with the business end of a reverse chrono-blaster held by Albert Einstein. Dipper ducks as the Nobel laureate fires, and the blast strikes a Time Pirate behind Dipper, turning the pirate into a baby. Dipper kicks the blaster out of Albert Einstein's hands, catches it, spins, and shoots the *T. rex*. The dinosaur immediately transforms into an adorable baby *T. rex* that looks like a large featherless parrot.

Mabel is quick to hop onto its back. "Charge, my little angel!" she says as she plows through a cadre of Time Pirates like they're bowling pins.

A bunch of them run away from her.

Big Ben rouses several of the Time Pirates and leads them into battle. They charge at Dipper, forcing him into a four-way swashbuckling sword fight. With their advanced clocksabers, they cut Dipper's sword down to nothing but a handle and knock him onto the sand.

"Yarrrgh, looks like the end of ye," says Big Ben. He draws back his clocksaber.

Dipper looks to Mabel and Blendin, who are in similar situations. Dipper feels around in the sand behind him, searching for something, anything. His hand grasps something solid. He draws it forward. It's a pickax.

"Yarrrgh, yourself!" yells Dipper. He swings the pickax, knocking the clocksaber from Big Ben's hand. Dipper looks at the shore. All manner of weird Old West things have washed up.

"Guys! There's a bunch of Old Western junk on the beach! Grab something!" he shouts.

Mabel grabs pies and starts throwing them at Time Pirates, causing them to shriek and flee. Blendin grabs a hoop dress and throws it over a Time Pirate's head before tackling him. Big Ben and the final contingent of Time Pirates retreat.

Dipper corrals them back toward their ship.

Blendin shoots more blaster fire and drives them away from his side.

Together, the three beat the Time Pirates back.

"What?" says Time Beard. "What's happening?"

"They're too powerful!" shouts a Time Pirate. "We can't stop them!"

"Darn tootin' you can't!" says Mabel.

Time Beard shakes his fist.

"Yarrrgh, you leave me no other choice," he says. "We have one last option."

All the Time Pirates shudder and murmur.

Big Ben approaches Time Beard. "You can't be serious!" he says.

"I am serious," says Time Beard. "RELEASE THE TIME CAT!"

Dipper and Mabel scrunch up their faces.

Blendin squeaks.

All the Time Pirates hide their eyes as an enormous door on the front of the galleon lowers. It hits the sand with a thud. A bloodcurdling growl emanates from the bowels of the ship. The ground shakes. Something very large steps forward from the shadows. Sensing it, the baby *T. rex* bolts off down the beach.

The twins draw what they're sure are going to be their final breaths.

Out from the ship steps an elephant-sized tabby cat.

"Awww, that's not so bad," says Mabel.

"MEEEOOOOOOOOAAAAAWWWRRRRRRRRRRRRR-RRRRRRRRRR!" the time cat roars, almost knocking Dipper and Mabel off their feet. It crouches.

All the twins can do is gulp.

"I guess we didn't m-make the r-right choice," stammers Dipper.

The time cat digs its claws into the sand and leaps toward Mabel!

The Time Pirates look away.

Then . . . the time cat rolls to a stop and starts pawing at Mabel's sweater.

"The ball of yarn on my sweater!" Mabel exclaims. "The time cat is mesmerized by it!"

The giant feline purrs and rolls around on its back.

The Time Pirates gasp.

"They fear not the time cat!" yells Calico Shorthand.

"The time cat fears not them!" yells Calico Longhand.

"Running is our only hope now!" yells Calico Secondhand.

All the Time Pirates start scrambling onto the ship. Some pull up the anchor and others cast the sails.

Time Beard roars, "Come back out here and fight! I am not moving my ship until—"

BOOM!

One of the Time Pirates punches Time Beard in the face.

"That Time Pirate just knocked his clocks out!" says Mabel.

"Mutiny!" shouts the Time Pirate as he drags their unconscious leader onto the ship.

Another Time Pirate grabs the helm and starts to steer the ship away.

Down on the beach the twins and Blendin cheer.

The time cat continues pawing at Mabel's sweater. It nuzzles up against her.

"We did it!" says Blendin. "We beat the Time Pirates! Can you believe this?"

"This is amazing!" says Mabel as she slips out of the yarn ball sweater. "And all because I happened to wear the right sweater!"

"Huh," says Dipper. "I guess that small choice did matter."

They survey the beach for a peaceful moment. It's blasted and charred from the battle with the Time Pirates, but the hyper-X remains.

Dipper and Mabel turn to Blendin. "Look, we're splitting this treasure three ways, just like we agreed," says Dipper, "because unlike Time Pirates, we're good for our word. But if you ever trick us again, so help us Time Baby, we're going to sic this time cat on you, you got it?"

Mabel snaps her fingers.

The beach shakes as the time cat growls at Blendin.

"G-g-got it!" stammers Blendin, gulping. "I'm really sorry, kids. I tried to make friends with the wrong crowd. Mabel, will you do the honors?" He hands Mabel a shovel.

Smiling, Mabel hits the hyper-X with the shovel, and treasure starts pouring out of it like coins in a video game.

There are rubies, gold coins, gold statues, famous paintings, a copy of the Declaration of Independence, Amelia Earhart looking very confused, and all sorts of riches.

Their jaws drop as they look at the haul.

"This is the biggest treasure I've ever seen!" says Dipper.

"Where am I?" asks Amelia.

"You could probably buy at least a boat with this!" says Mabel as she picks up a handful of coins and drops them on her own head.

Dipper and Mabel dance, but Blendin stares at the treasure and and thinks.

"I have an idea," says Blendin. "Kids, this treasure is just a drop in the bucket. If we wanted to, with this time cat, we could take over the Time Pirate crew and travel the ages looting twice as much. Why be *rich* when we can be *double* rich?"

"I dunno," says Mabel. "Doesn't that seem a little greedy?"

"It's been a long day and maybe we should just be content with the infinite wealth that's already in our hands," says Dipper as coins continue to flow from the hyper-X like a fountain.

"Come on, guys, be greedy with me!" says Blendin as he waves around the time tape in his hands. "There's nothing wrong with that! Eh? Eh? I pull this, we go back a few minutes and take over the Time Pirates' ship before they can leave? DOUBLE RICH."

Dipper and Mabel look at each other.

"Which should we choose?" asks Mabel.

TO BE GREEDY: GO TO PAGE 210

NOT TO BE GREEDY: GO TO PAGE 240

GO AFTER THE TREASURE

"**T**his is a no-brainer!" Mabel says, smiling.

"I guess I *have* always wanted an infinite pile of treasure," says Dipper.

"Plus it would be fun paying Grunkle Stan to do embarrassing things!" says Mabel. "But how do we get it?"

"A Time Pirate has hidden the treasure beneath a hyper-X on a time island in a time ocean that you can only reach by entering a specific time portal," says Blendin.

"Is, like, someone paying you every time you say the word *time*?" asks Mabel.

"Pay time attention!" Blendin yells. "The only way to enter that portal is to find a key. And yes, it's a *Time Key*, Miss Know-It-All!" Blendin shoots Mabel a glare, then unfurls an old map with an illustration of a key.

Dipper's and Mabel's eyes widen.

"Time Keys are extremely rare, but if we find just one, that treasure is as good as ours! I've tracked down its general location. It's either in medieval England . . . or lost somewhere in the Old West . . . or it's supposed to be here." Blendin holds out the map to show Dipper.

Dipper looks at it and laughs. "Well, there's your problem, Blendo!" he says. "You've got the right place but the wrong time." Dipper flips the map upside down and shows Blendin where it says 20705. "The key may be in the future!"

Blendin groans. "Ugh, my mom was right. I really am bad at everything I try." He takes out his time tape.

"Ooooh," says Mabel. "Three adventures to choose from? Each more exciting than the last? My goodness!"

"Don't make this decision lightly," says Blendin. "This isn't just fun and games. Each of those places has some serious dangers. Medieval England is probably going to give us the plague. In the future, we'll be hunted outlaws, and the part of the West we'd have to go to was ruled by the Calamity Brothers, history's most dangerous bandits!"

"Psssh, all I'm hearing is 'dragons, space races, and mining adventures'!" says Mabel.

"We have to pick one," says Dipper. "But which one?"

THE WILD WEST: GO TO PAGE 131

THE FUTURE: GO TO PAGE 190

MEDIEVAL TIMES: GO TO PAGE 219

TALK TO THE DRAGON

"**W**ait, guys!" says Mabel. "Can't you see he's in pain?" She turns to the dragon and approaches it. "Be still, dragon friend. Let Mabel heal you with her words."

"Do . . . do you mean it?" asks the dragon.

"Don't worry about me. Let's talk about *you*," says Mabel.

The dragon smiles and lies down as Mabel pulls out a notepad. "Okay, well I guess it all started in elementary school," says the dragon. "The other dragons always picked me last for dragon ball. . . ."

An hour passes and the dragon and Mabel are holding each other, with the dragon crying into her shoulder.

Dipper and Blendin roll their eyes and flip gold coins in a corner to pass the time.

"So I told him, 'I don't want to incinerate people for food,'" the dragon says to Mabel. "'I wanna go to art school, Dad!'" He wipes a tear from his eye. "And he said, 'Well then, you must not be my son. 'Cause no son of mine would be an artist. Do you know how hard it is to find a job? You'll probably end up writing children's books instead!'"

"And how did that make you feel?" asks Mabel.

"It made me feel small! And . . . and unloved!" cries the dragon.

"There, there, Connerheart the Dragon. It's okay. But it's time to seize the future! Which means you've gotta let go of the past. You can trust me. I'm a time-traveling twelve-year-old girl."

Connerheart smiles. "Mabel, this was the most productive conversation I've ever had in my life. I don't even wanna eat your bones anymore. Is there anything I can do to repay you?"

"Well, we're trying to get a key from the king, and he said he'd give it to us if we brought him back the goblet you stole," says Mabel.

"This old thing?" asks Connerheart, pulling a goblet out from under a dwarf's skeleton. "It's all yours! You know, the treasure in here isn't even real gold. It's just wooden coins and items painted gold. It makes for a rather fanciful aesthetic, if I can say so myself. But I digress. You should probably know that you've been lied to!"

"What?" asks Mabel.

"This was never even the king's goblet. He's just been sending people here for years to 'get it back' as a distraction. It's how he gets rid of unwanted trespassers."

Dipper and Blendin drop their coins, mouths agape.

"The king probably offered you one of three challenges, didn't he?" says the dragon.

Everyone gasps.

"He did, I knew it!" says the dragon. "Always with the challenges."

"Okay, maybe, on second thought," says Mabel, "how about you fly us to the castle and help give that king a talking to!"

"Ho-ho, you mean vengeance?" says the dragon. "But how can you *seize the future* if you're still holding on to vengeful feelings?" He smiles.

"THE FUTURE IS VENGEANCE," says Mabel.

"Are you sure?" asks Dipper.

"YES, I'M SURE I WANT VENGEANCE!" says Mabel.

TO BE VENGEFUL: GO TO PAGE 41

NOT TO BE VENGEFUL: GO TO PAGE 183

MABEL DRIVES

"**Uh, uh, uh . . . I'm gonna go with Mabel on this!**" says Blendin. "She's louder and more annoying and I personally respect that."

"YES!" Mabel says with a pump of her fist.

"All right, I'm the captain of this here time ship, and as such I want everyone to refer to me as Madam Captain," she says.

Blendin nods.

Dipper rolls his eyes.

"We've got an insane race ahead of us, but by the grace of Time Baby, we're going to win. I guarantee it," says Mabel with a smack of her fist in her palm. "Dipper, you're my copilot. Blendin, you watch from the stands and radio us help if we need it." Mabel tosses Blendin a radio from a nearby gear closet. "LET'S RACE!"

At the starting line, Mabel fires up the engine.

The entire craft rumbles and pulses with an electric glow.

"Yeah, baby! We got some power here!" Mabel says. "Who needs puncture-proof fuel tanks when you're riding lightning?" She revs the engines.

Strange alien racers climb into their vehicles. The dust settles on the track.

A space racer with the name *Racer T* speeds toward them.

"Oh, m-man, it's *Racer T!*" stammers Blendin through the intercom. "Its pilot is the fiercest space racer who ever lived! His dirty tricks are uglier than his hideous alien face!"

The racer pulls right up next to them.

Dipper, Mabel, and Blendin scream when they see . . .

"TOBY DETERMINED?" the trio exclaim.

Sure enough, the pilot navigating *Racer T* is their hometown reporter and social outcast, Toby Determined.

"What are you doing here?" asks Dipper.

"Well, I accidentally fell into a time portal while I was trying to use the public showers at the pool," says Toby. "When I got here, people automatically assumed I was an alien and let me do whatever I wanted. Turns out I have a knack for racing. All that time following Shandra Jimenez in my car really paid off!"

"Toby, can you let us win this race, please?" asks Mabel. "We'll give you a cut of our treasure!"

"Yeah, right!" says Toby. "I'm the official racer of Emperor Snorgshnog now and make time-millions in sponsorships! You little twerps are going down! Ha-cha-cha!" He puts on his helmet and lowers the visor.

Mabel glowers. "*He's* going down," she says.

"IT'S TIME FOR THE RACE TO BEGIN!" yells the announcer.

Ahead of them, the signal light flashes.

It goes red.

Yellow.

Indigo.

Binary.

Kaleidoscope.

Green.

Mabel floors the pedal and takes off with a sonic BOOM!

The crowd goes insane.

The twins are off to an early lead, with Toby Determined closely trailing them. They're moving at impossible speeds, but Mabel is dodging stone arches and stalagmites, weaving through the canyon with grace.

The g-forces blow Dipper's cheeks back to his ears. "MAAAAAABELLLLLL . . . we're going tooooo faaaasssst."

"You're amazing!" says Blendin over the intercom. "How can a kid from the past even think fast enough to keep up with these turns?"

"I eat sugar straight out of the box!" screams Mabel, her smile widening.

On a wide turn, Toby Determined cuts the corner to catch up and starts ramming the side of the twins' racer, trying to knock them off course. Laughing annoyingly, he hits his afterburners, temporarily blinding the twins with the jet-fire flash from his engines.

Mabel radios Blendin. "Blendin! He's taken the lead! What should we do?"

"It looks like you guys are coming up on the Boonta Roku S curve!" says Blendin. "Just before it, to your left, is a secret passage. It's a shortcut and it'll give you the lead!"

"Isn't that cheating?" screams Mabel.

"Does it matter?" Blendin yells back.

"Ah, jeez, what do we do, Dipper?" she asks. "We have to decide quickly! Should we take the passage and cheat to win? Or should I pause to consider the ethics and then cheat anyway?"

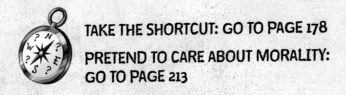

TAKE THE SHORTCUT: GO TO PAGE 178

PRETEND TO CARE ABOUT MORALITY: GO TO PAGE 213

ACCEPT THE MARRIAGE

"**I**'ll do it!" **says Dipper.** "I'll marry your daughter!"

Mabel gasps and pulls him and Blendin aside. "Dipper, what are you doing? This is *love* you're toying with."

"Don't worry," says Dipper. "It's just a formality. I say yes, maybe he'll give us the key, and then we can run away before they complete the ceremony. Trust me. There's nothing that could actually make me go through with thi—"

"WENDINELLA!" shouts the king. "Come meet your husband!"

With the heralding of trumpets, a tall, freckled redhead steps into the courtyard.

"'Sup, dude?" says Wendinella.

Dipper's jaw drops. "Wendy?" he says.

"Wendinella, speak appropriately, please," says the king. "Your choice of words confuses my ear!" He leans toward Dipper, Mabel, and Blendin. "Teenagers, amiright?"

Blendin nods.

Wendinella rolls her eyes. "So are you, like, my husband? Let's get on with this, dude. I can't wait to get out of this town!"

"Out of this town?" asks Dipper.

"Yeah, don't you know? After the ceremony, we're given our own castle and kingdom and whatever. We even get serfs! I'm gonna make 'em form human pyramids and arm wrestle for my amusement."

"That sounds amazing," mutters Dipper, wide-eyed and smiling.

The king steps down from his balcony throne and approaches Dipper. "Well, considering you're about to be my kin, I suppose I might as well give you this." He hands Dipper the Time Key that they've been searching for.

Mabel's and Blendin's eyes go wide.

Dipper looks at them, then back at Wendinella, who's staring lovingly at him.

Mabel holds up the time tape, as if to suggest they should take this opportunity and run.

Dipper gulps.

"Oh, no," says Mabel as she pulls Dipper in for a huddle. "You're actually thinking about going through with it, aren't you?"

"Mabel. This is everything I've ever wanted. This

princess is basically Wendy. I'd have my own land. I'd be able to study alchemy and dragons with the girl of my dreams!"

"Yeah, in the Middle Ages! There aren't even dentists!" says Mabel.

"I hate dentists!" says Dipper.

The king coughs. "Ahem, the marriage ceremony?"

Dipper looks at Wendinella, who seems like a dream.

"It's your life, Dipper, but I would strongly recommend not staying here," says Mabel.

Dipper thinks about it.

GO THROUGH WITH THE MARRIAGE: GO TO PAGE 89

WALK AWAY FROM THE ALTAR: GO TO PAGE 176

GOLD POTION

"**I** think we'll take the—" says Mabel.

"GOLD! GOLD! GOLD!" screams Blendin.

Dipper and Mabel stare at him.

"What?" says Blendin. "That's why we went on this whole stupid adventure in the first place!"

"I can't argue with that!" shrugs Mabel. "Imagine if stuff you touched turned to gold! Everything would be amazing! Except for playing basketball, come to think of it."

"Yeah," says Dipper. "I guess it would be neat to turn people into gold statues."

"SO BE IT!" says the wizard as he hands the gang a flask of glowing gold liquid. He then mounts a unicorn and rides off into the sunset, like you do.

Blendin pops the cap off the flask and takes a swig. He passes it to Dipper, who does the same. Dipper passes it to Mabel, who wipes off the rim and then also swigs.

"Does anyone feel any different?" she asks.

Everyone shrugs.

Dipper touches a rock with his finger and watches it turn to gold. "WHOA! It worked! Guys, we have the power! High-five!"

They all lean back to high-five and then—

"Wait!" screams Blendin. "We almost all high-fived each other into being gold statues."

"Phew, that would have been really dumb. Good catch!" Mabel says as they all simultaneously wipe their brows in relief and turn themselves to gold.

 THE END

DIPPER DRIVES

"**U**h . . . I choose Dipper!" says Blendin.

Mabel throws down her helmet and scowls.

"Sorry, he's glaring at me and I don't like confrontation!" says Blendin. He scampers off to the stands.

"Well, it's decided. Let's hop in this bad boy and take it out," says Dipper. He climbs into the pilot's seat and Mabel scoops up her helmet and settles into the copilot's seat beside him.

A pit crew begins to push Dipper's craft toward the starting line, where strange alien racers are getting into their vehicles and revving their engines.

"IT'S ALMOST TIME FOR THE RACE TO BEGIN!" comes the announcement through the loudspeakers. "ALL RISE FOR OUR NATIONAL ANTHEM, AN ANCIENT SONG WE'VE BEEN SINGING FOR THOUSANDS OF YEARS!"

Everyone in the stands rises to their feet. "ARE WE BLANCHIN', GIRL, WE'RE BLANCHIN'. I LIVE UP IN A MANSION," they chant in unison, hands over their hearts.

"This is truly a terrible time," says Dipper.

"Are you sure you can pilot this thing?" asks Mabel. "It looks pretty complicated, and you get overconfident sometimes."

Dipper peers at the controls, which consist of hundreds

of buttons, dials, and switches marked with alien symbols. One button just has a picture of a dog on it.

"Maybe try that button! What about that button?" says Mabel.

"Mabel, cut it out," says Dipper. "No one likes a backseat driver."

"Hey, Dipper," says Blendin over the intercom. "I'm going to be your backseat driver. Hopefully you don't mind me and your sister talking constantly while you drive."

"Guys, seriously, both of you, I've got this!" says Dipper.

"READY . . ." says the announcer.

Alien racers rev their engines.

"SET . . ."

Dipper grips the wheel and stares at the controls.

"GO!"

Dipper presses a big green button.

WHOOOSH!

The carriage rushes . . . backward.

Dipper and Mabel scream. The racer zooms in reverse faster than anything they've ever seen before.

"You pressed the wrong button!" screams Mabel. "I knew I should have driven!"

"I just want to take this moment to remind everyone about seat belt safety," says Blendin.

"How is that useful right now?" screams Dipper.

Their racer stops.

"Whew, you stopped it!" says Mabel.

"Mabel," says Dipper, brow furrowing, "I didn't press anything."

The twins look out the racer in terror to see that Time Baby is holding them in his massive chubby fingers.

"YOUR POOR RACING HAS DISPLEASED TIME BABY," he says, his voice booming like thunder. "YOU WILL MAKE FINE NUM-NUMS FOR MY ENORMOUS BELLY."

He tilts the racer toward his mouth and begins to devour it.

"Oh, man, sorry about this, guys," says Blendin over the intercom. "On the bright side, it's an incredible honor to be eaten by Time Baby."

Time Baby gums their racer and giggles.

It's definitely adorable.
All things considered, there are
worse ways to meet your . . .

 **END.**

AGREE TO THE SHOOT-OUT WITH WILD EYES JOE

"**I**'ll do it!" **shouts Dipper** as he wrests himself free from Wild Eyes Joe's grip. "Just leave my friends and me alone! And stop drooling so much," he adds. "Spittoons are basically, like, everywhere, man. Just use 'em."

Wild Eyes Joe smirks. "Well, maybe you're not such a coward after all!" He spits at one of the pots and misses, then drags Dipper outside into the dusty town square.

The rustle of people coming and going fades out as the townsfolk scurry inside buildings, dive behind horses, and hide in barrels. Vultures begin circling overhead.

Mabel squints her eyes and raises her hand to her face like a visor. "Man, the sun sure is high in the sky at noon," she says. "Wait a minute. . . ." Mabel points a finger at the sun. "Ha-ha! I get what you're doing there, sun!"

Wild Eyes Joe draws a line in the sand with his foot and says, "Duelin' rules are simple. Start here, walk about forty paces, then DRAW!"

"*About* forty paces?" asks Dipper. "Shouldn't we have an exact number?"

"Hey, boys, Copernicus here wants an exact number!" shouts Wild Eyes Joe, with a hearty laugh.

"Who's Copernicus?" asks one squeaky-voiced tooth-less outlaw.

Without blinking, Wild Eyes Joe whips out his weapon and shoots at the outlaw, barely missing him as he ducks behind a water trough. Everyone hushes.

"ANY MORE SMART-GUY QUESTIONS?" shouts Wild Eyes Joe.

Dipper gulps. "Uhhh, one, actually," he says. "I, uh . . . don't have a weapon."

"You don't have a weapon?" says Wild Eyes Joe. "This is the West! Even babies have weapons out here! In fact, they're required to by law!"

Dipper opens his mouth, but Blendin pulls him aside out of earshot of the townsfolk.

"Look, I brought two laser blasters from the future, remember?" Blendin whispers. "Just use one of them!"

"That's great!" says Dipper. "I was, uh, really not looking forward to killing anyone."

"There's only one problem," says Blendin. "The blasters got pretty banged up from traveling, so . . . one might be a bit unstable now. Oops."

"How can you possibly be this bad at your job, Blendin?" asks Dipper.

"It took a lot of time and practice!" says Blendin with a smile.

Dipper takes a look at the two blasters in Blendin's hands.

Which blaster should Dipper use?

THE LONG AND SKINNY BLASTER:
GO TO PAGE 180

THE SHORT AND FAT BLASTER:
GO TO PAGE 159

OPEN THE DOORS TO THE TREASURE ROOM

The gang pushes open the sturdy oak doors.

"Man, when we finally get to that treasure, I'm gonna swim in it," says Mabel. "I don't care if it's physically impossible!"

"I'm gonna rub the treasure on my face and make weirdly uncomfortable moaning sounds for a very long time!" says Blendin. "So heads up about that."

The door gives way, and Blendin waves the torch.

A single pedestal stands in the middle of the room.

"That must be it! That must be where the Time Key is!" says Dipper.

They approach it, shaking. Blendin reaches out.

"What? Where is it?" he asks.

"And why is there a note?" asks Mabel.

"Guys, I think someone got to the Time Key before we could," says Dipper, picking up the note. He reads it out loud: "'To whom it may concern: I, famed gambler Chazforth Bumpkinfudder of Kenosha, Wisconsin, have taken this key and gone back to town to try to sell it. To be honest, I don't know what it's for or why I'm even leaving this note. Good day!'"

"Awww, man, I knew this was too good to be true," says Blendin.

"Wait!" says Dipper. He inspects the paper. "He says he's a gambler. That probably means that he gave the key to those outlaws we saw playing cards!" He looks from Blendin to Mabel. "We have to go to the card game!"

"Awww, nuts," says Blendin. "I don't like things when they're difficult."

"Just think of how good your life is gonna be when we finally get this treasure!" says Dipper.

"Think of how much better *all* our lives will be," says Mabel. "Let's go back to town and try one of those other leads. Pines Force Five!"

"There are three of us," says Dipper.

They all put their hands in a circle and cheer before rushing back to town. Dipper feels more determined than ever to get the key as they head off to . . .

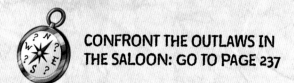

CONFRONT THE OUTLAWS IN THE SALOON: GO TO PAGE 237

WAND-ER AROUND

The Pitt Cola fills the chamber.

Dipper, Mabel, and Blendin flounder and face the wizard.

"The a-answer is," Blendin stammers, "that he *wandered around?*"

The wizard stares into Blendin's eyes. "IMPOSSIBLE!" he screams. "Curse my own rules!" He claps his hands and the Pitt Cola begins draining from the room.

The gang floats back down to the soda-drenched dungeon floor.

"Ewww, my feet are stuck to the ground," Mabel says.

All around the room, things are askew and stuck to other things.

"Well, you've survived my death trap," says the wizard, shrugging. "So, what brings you here?"

"The king sent us to bring you back," says Dipper.

"What? Never! You can't take me back to that slave-driver!" screams the wizard. "He makes me dance for his amusement, and he consolidates all of his employees' birthdays into one wretched office party. It's terrible!" Just awful!

"Awww, we know how you feel," says Mabel. "Our Grunkle Stan makes us work all day in a gift shop. It's mostly horsing around and eating popsicles in an air-conditioned room, but it's still annoying, you know."

"I never wanted to be a wizard anyway!" he laments. "I wanted to be a confectioner and make fizzy sodas that tickle the inside of my nose and make my heart giggle!"

"Ah, that explains all the weird soda stuff," says Mabel, slowly nodding. "I was wondering how that was going to pay off."

"Please, you can't take me back. Please just go and tell the king that something horrible happened to me! Like I died or started taking improv classes! Just let me go!" pleads the wizard.

Dipper, Mabel, and Blendin huddle up.

"I dunno, guys," says Dipper. "Us getting that treasure depends on us bringing this guy back."

"But, Dipper, look at him!" says Mabel, gesturing. "He's a man with dreams. Weirdly specific soda-making dreams!"

The trio thinks long and hard.

LET THE WIZARD GO: GO TO PAGE 55

TAKE THE WIZARD TO THE KING: GO TO PAGE 62

JOIN DAVY AND FIGHT THE COPS

Dipper exhales, looks into Davy Time-Jones's watering clock eye, and says, "Clock Kings for life, bro." He drops down, kicks, and sweeps Lolph's legs out from under him.

Davy Time-Jones smiles. He grabs Dundgren by the arm and flips him over his head! He takes Dundgren's blaster and lays suppressing fire, forcing the other Time Anomaly Enforcement Agents to hit the ground and cover their heads. Dipper, Mabel, and Blendin follow Davy. He pulls the pin on a time grenade strapped to Dundgren's chest before pushing him over to his comrades and running away with the trio.

Behind them, an explosion sounds and babies dressed like Time Anomaly Enforcement Agents fly everywhere.

When the group gets safely away, Davy Time-Jones kneels and addresses Dipper. "Dipper, I knew you weren't a cop," he says. "You have too much heart. Also, your name is really dumb. They would never allow that on the force."

"Please, it's nothing, Davy Time-Jones," says Dipper, bowing.

"No, no, I owe you my life," says Davy. "The Time Key you seek . . . I know who has it. His name is Dos Hunthou, and he's being kept as an indentured servant to a wealthy space racer. Find him, set him free, and he will give you the key."

"Thanks, Davy Time-Jones," says Dipper.

"No, thank *you*," says Davy Time-Jones. "And your sister and your giant man-baby, also."

Davy Time-Jones throws a saddle on the back of an enormous two-headed Komodo dragon and rides into the sunset, finally a free man.

Dipper, Mabel, and Blendin watch him go.

"He was the best of us . . . and the worst of us," says Blendin.

"A scoundrel, but a hero," says Mabel. "What was he in prison for again?"

"He burned down a *lot* of hospitals," says Blendin.

"Huh," says Mabel. "Maybe—maybe we shouldn't have helped him escape."

Dipper and Blendin look at her and start to nod.

"Oh, well," says Mabel. "Too late now!" She waves her sweater sleeves. "Ready to get that Time Key?"

"There's only one way to free Dos Hunthou," says Dipper. "Who's ready for a space race?"

 SPACE RACE: GO TO PAGE 223

THE WILD WEST

"**T**he Oooolllllld West!" Mabel shouts. She spits on the ground.

Dipper fires imaginary six-shooters into the air.

"Okay, guys," says Blendin. "That seems as good a place as any to find the key! Hold on to your hats. We're traveling through time *and* space, so things might get illogical!" Blendin pulls the time tape, and with an electric surge—

WHOOOOSH!

—they appear in a distant town.

Then the buildings around them shrink in fast motion, clouds whip through the sky, cacti rise from the earth, and in a blinding flash of light, they find themselves standing on the rough-and-tumble dirt streets of an old town: Calamity Junction.

"Whoa!" exclaims Mabel.

"Neat!" shouts Dipper.

"Watch out!" yells Blendin, tackling the twins.

A stagecoach races through the spot where they were just standing.

"We gotta be careful!" says Blendin, coughing up dust, sand, and a rusty bullet.

"I can't believe it!" says Dipper. "The Wild, Wild West!"

Mabel squints at him. "Ehhh, I dunno. It's wild all right, but is it *wild*, wild?"

SMASH!

A black-vested desperado is thrown from a second-story saloon window. He lands on a grazing buffalo, is bucked off, careens through a cactus patch, and smashes into the double doors of another saloon. The passing townsfolk don't even turn their heads as they walk by.

Mabel grins. "Wiiiiild, wiiiild," she whispers.

"Well, the first thing we should do is find a way to blend in," says Dipper.

"Lucky for you, that's my middle name!" says Blendin.

"Actually, it's your first," says Dipper. "Anyway, I don't like the way these townsfolk are looking at us." Dipper motions to a group of townspeople staring them down and pointing.

Dipper, Mabel, and Blendin stroll into a nearby general store to find a change of clothes. The place is a ramshackle affair, not unlike the Mystery Shack. There are rows and rows of chicken feed and gold-panning supplies, as well as antiquated foods like johnnycakes and corn dodgers. Behind the counter sits a familiar-looking hayseed type who seems an awful lot like the farmer back in Gravity Falls.

"Farmer Sprott?" asks Dipper. "What are you doing way out here?"

"Nay, I'm not a farmer, but my last name is Sprott," he says. "People call me Shopkeeper Sprott, sure enough. And judging by the looks of your clothing, y'all must be witches!" Slowly, he pulls a pitchfork from behind the counter.

"Ha-ha, uh, no. We're, uh . . . from the city," says Mabel with an awkward sideways glance.

"*Witch* City?" he asks, narrowing his eyes at her.

"Which city, indeed," says Mabel.

Nodding slowly, Shopkeeper Sprott puts down the pitchfork. "Well, your wordplay tricks have me plumb distracted," he says. "What brings y'all 'round these parts?"

"We're looking for a magic key so I can dress my pig in gold!" says Mabel with a huge grin.

Dipper steps in front of her. "Forget that!" he says. "It's a normal key. A good ol' worthless key nobody would ever want."

"But we want it!" says Blendin, who's sweating. "Boy, do we ever want it."

Shopkeeper Sprott reaches slowly for the pitchfork.

"No, no, wait!" Dipper says. He unfurls the map. "It looks like this!"

Shopkeeper Sprott looks at it and nods. "I saw a man with such a key! He was wearing all manner of puffy exotic clothing and said *'ARRR'* a lot, sure enough. I think he lost that key in a card game with the outlaws who terrorize yonder saloon!" He motions to the saloon across the way, where several villainous-looking cowboys sit seedily around a card table.

Dipper, Mabel, and Blendin gulp.

A woman steps beside the shopkeeper and says to him, "Oh, hush, Ezekiel." She turns to their present company. "That pirate stranger didn't lose the key in a card game! He traded it to that wily prospector on the outskirts of town. You should go to the old mine if you wanna find it."

"You're both wrong!" says a man with short shorts and a mustache. "I saw that man leave town on the last train. *With the key!* But there ain't no way to get it now 'cept train robbin'!"

Dipper, Mabel, and Blendin each pick out their favorite cowboy attire, pay at the counter, and step outside the general store.

"All three of these leads make sense," says Dipper. "Whaddya think, guys? Should we confront those mean-looking cowboys, or should we poke around in the old mine? The train has already left town, so if we go after it, we'll have to take horses and ride up like an old-fashioned train robbery!"

"Horses!" says Mabel. "Anything with horses!"

CONFRONT THE OUTLAWS IN THE SALOON: GO TO PAGE 237

COMMIT A GREAT TRAIN ROBBERY: GO TO PAGE 37

EMBARK ON A MINING ADVENTURE: GO TO PAGE 255

TURN DOWN TOBY'S OFFER AND LEAVE HIM

"**S**orry, Toby," says Dipper. "No one wants to be around you."

"It's true!" says Blendin.

"Oh, fiddlesticks!" says Toby.

"Don't worry!" says Mabel. "I'm sure in some parallel time line someone is helping you out right now. Not us, though! And I'm *sure* we made the right choice this time!"

✦ ✦✦ ✦

They walk for almost an hour through dark twisting passages.

"W-which way are we going?" asks Blendin.

"Yeah, haven't we passed this skeleton before?" says Mabel. "And how many times have we gone down this hall?"

"Hey . . . guys?" says Dipper, wiping his forehead. "Didn't the king say that this dungeon was an endless maze, and that we'd go completely insane down here?"

"That's ridiculous!" says Mabel. "I feel as sane as ever! Don't you agree, giant hovering rainbow-colored duck?"

"I DO AGREE!" quacks the kaleidoscopic duck. "AND I SAY THAT WE ALL MUST DANCE!"

"YES!" screams Blendin, manically ripping off his shirt. "LET US DANCE!"

The trio starts dancing to imaginary disco lights and music.

They've gone completely insane.

They might be having fun, but for our adventurers, it looks like . . .

 **THE END.**

TAKE THE CONDUCTOR HOSTAGE

"**I**'ve had enough of this!" Mabel screams. She grabs the conductor by the collar of his coat. "We're criminals, and we're taking over this train!" She shoves the conductor to his knees and then whispers in his ear. "Don't be afraid, we're mostly kidding. But if you try to run, I will *drop* you, grandpa!"

The conductor pulls the bell cord, signaling for the engineer to stop.

The train skids to a halt. Passengers get riled up.

"Mabel? Have you lost your mind?" shouts Dipper.

"Instinct took over. There's no turning back now. Here, cover me," whispers Mabel, reaching into her pocket and tossing him Blendin's laser blaster.

Dipper grabs it and waves it at the passengers. "Stay—stay back!" he stammers. "I have a weird future blaster that misfires a LOT!"

Passengers cower and shriek.

"Seriously, how do I use this?" says Dipper.

Mabel guides the conductor to the restricted railcar. "All right, bub, open that door if you don't want trouble!" She drops her voice to a whisper and smiles. "You're doing a really good job."

The conductor begins to unlock the safe.

There's a blast from the passenger car.

Mabel runs back in to see what's happening.

Dipper has accidentally fired the laser blaster and the beam ricochets through the train. Passengers scream, gasp, and duck, shielding their faces.

Dipper's hat and poncho burn up, and Mabel's bonnet and prairie dress ignite.

"Get this off of me!" she shouts, shaking off the fiery dress.

The laser bounces into the cargo hold and disintegrates the keys in the conductor's hand.

"FREEZE AND COME OUT WITH YOUR HANDS UP!" someone shouts.

Dipper and Mabel approach the window. The train is surrounded by lawmen.

"What do we do, what do we do?" asks Mabel.

"If you surrender, we won't hurt you!" says the sheriff. "We'll just jail you forever! And *possibly* hurt you!"

Dipper and Mabel look at each other.

"Mabel, is this the end of the line?" asks Dipper.

"I don't know!" says Mabel. "Should we turn ourselves in or try to make a run for it?"

SURRENDER: GO TO PAGE 207

MAKE A RUN FOR IT: GO TO PAGE 227

FOLLOW TOBY THROUGH THE DUNGEON

"**U**gh! All right, Mabel," says Dipper. "But if Toby asks me to sniff his dungeon rags again, we're gonna ditch him."

"Yay!" says Mabel. "Toby, you're coming with us. Show us the way!"

"Yippee!" says Toby. "You won't regret this, you guys. I'm a pro at these tunnels." With a smile, Toby leads them down the corridor toward a flickering light coming through a doorway. "I think the wizard should be in here!" he exclaims. "I've heard a lot of curses coming from this hallway. The swear kind *and* the magic kind!"

The trio murmurs, nodding and smiling.

"You three go ahead without me! I'm going to enjoy roaming these caverns for more delicious cave fish, ha-cha-cha!"

The gang bids farewell to Toby and rushes down the winding corridor, entering a three-story chamber lined with bookshelves. In the middle sits an enormous table.

In the corner is a large desk covered with various inventions and writings. In another corner is a simmering cauldron with a sparkling mist frothing over its lip.

"Could this be the wizard's lair?" asks Mabel.

Blendin picks up a parchment scroll.

It reads:

ON WIZARDING.
A WIZARD'S GUIDE TO
WIZZY WHAMMING AND WIZ-ZIZZLING:
BY WIZARD THE WIZARD

"I dunno," says Blendin. "Jury's still out on this one."

"We made it!" says Dipper. "But where's the wizard?"

"Where, win-deed?" adds Mabel.

"Well, he's been here recently," says Dipper, gesturing to a half-eaten hock of ham. "So recently, in fact, it's almost suspicious he's not here now."

Mabel stops listening when she spies a giant golden goblet brimming with a fizzy, delicious-looking drink. A sign below it reads: YON COLA OF PITTS. PLEASE TRY. Mabel reaches for the goblet.

"Uh, Mabel, doesn't that seem a little suspicious?" asks Dipper. "You know. Like it was left there on purpose? Like a trap?"

"Please, Dipper, he's clearly left soda out for thirsty strangers who stumble into his home. It's just good hospitality!" She clutches the goblet and lifts it. But the goblet doesn't lift. It's affixed to a lever that slams the doors shut, and suddenly, fizzy Pitt Cola starts pouring out of ornate openings in the wall. The room is filling up quick.

"AH, what do we do, what do we do?" yells Blendin.

"It's fizzy! And the bubbles burn my nose!" yells Dipper.

"Yeah, I guess you could say this is a *sticky* situation," adds Mabel.

"Stop making puns, Mabel!" shouts Dipper. "Puns have literally never helped anyone ever!"

Suddenly, malevolent cackling fills the room, and with a puff of smoke a wizard appears above them, levitating near the ceiling. "Welcome to my workshop, foolish mortals! My workshop of ironic death!" He cackles again.

"Why are you doing this?" screams Mabel.

"Because no one can bring me back to that snooty king!" He laughs. "Unless, of course, you answer my riddle, whereby I am required by the wizard's code to set you free!"

"Okay. So. Let's do that!" says Mabel.

"Okay, okay, okay, but this is fiendishly clever!" says the wizard, cackling.

"JUST TELL US!" yells Mabel. "My hair is getting sticky and gross!"

"Okay," says the wizard, snickering. "What did the wizard do at the wizard convention at the wizard hotel?"

"I know this one!" says Mabel. "He *wand*-ered around," she whispers to Dipper.

"I dunno, Mabel, are you sure? I think the answer might be that he ordered *broom* service. What do you think, Blendin? Did he *wand*-er around or order *broom* service?"

"Ahhh, ahhh, jeez," says Blendin. "They're both stupid enough to be right!"

"Tick-tock!" says the wizard.

The room is almost full of fizzy soda.

"Blendin, you have to answer!" says Mabel.

WAND-ER AROUND: GO TO PAGE 125

BROOM SERVICE: GO TO PAGE 77

TRAVEL TO THE TREASURE

The twins feel the familiar electric sensation as they dissolve into the time stream. But just before the time tape fully retracts, Blendin grabs it between his fingers, holding it. Suddenly, the whole group stops still in the middle of a glowing blue tunnel of energy and light. Clocks and calendars float past them. Mabel looks into the wall and sees various historical events happening, as if they're on strips of film. Scenes from their summer play out before them. Dipper tries to cover a reel of him doing the Lamby Lamby Dance.

"We're in the middle of the time stream!" says Blendin, looking around. "Hopefully in the right place . . . Aha!" he says, pointing over the twins' shoulders.

There, in the middle of the Wall of Time, is a round door with a skull and crossbones painted on it and an ancient keyhole in the middle. Blendin produces the Time Key, inserts it into the hole, and turns.

Dipper and Mabel hold their breath.

CLICK!

The door swings open.

On the other side, in stark contrast to the rushing time surge they're standing in, is a serene tropical island. They all step through the door and fall into the sand.

"Ah, jeez, *why?*" says Mabel as she pulls a giant crab out of her hair.

They turn around and look up at the magical doorway floating six feet above the sand.

"Welcome to Time Island!" says Blendin. "Just have to mark the location so I don't lose it." He presses a button on his wrist locator, which beeps. "There. Now, somewhere here is a hyper-X, under which is the legendary Time Pirates' Treasure!"

"Oooh," says Mabel. "What's a hyper-X look like?"

"Is that it?" asks Dipper, pointing to a glowing, constantly morphing X that looks like it exists in more than one dimension.

"It is!" yells Blendin with a smile as he grabs a shovel and skips toward it.

"This is the end of all our troubles! Anything we desire!" he shouts.

"Infinite sweaters!" exclaims Mabel.

"My own observatory! And beard implants!" says Dipper.

Blendin lifts the shovel above the sand.

A noise breaks through the air. It sounds like . . . ticking. First it's soft; then it grows louder. Then there's a gong like a grandfather clock and, suddenly—

BLAST!

The entire beach is lit up by a neon-green explosion behind them.

A gruff voice calls out, "TIME'S UP, MATEY!"

They spin around to see something coming out of a giant green time portal: it's a massive hovering Spanish galleon filled with a motley band of dastardly Time Pirates, with all manners of clocks and gears sticking out of their beards. One rides a *T. rex*.

"*Time Pirates?*" yells Mabel.

"THAT BE US!" bellows the captain. "Behold my dastardly crew! Meet Long Time Silver, Scurvy Stopwatch Sam, Tony Tick-Tock, Green Gears, Calico Shorthand, Calico Longhand, Calico Secondhand, and Big Ben!"

"Yarrrrrrghhh," snarl the pirates, raising their clock-sabers and leaping from the ship onto the sand as the captain looks on from the ship.

Big Ben smiles and chimes like a clock.

"And I'm the one they call Time Beard," says the captain, gesturing to the many clocks tangled in his beard. "But you already know that, don't you, Blendin Blandin?" He hops into the sand.

"Wait, they know you? What's going on here?" asks Mabel.

Blendin blushes. Then he approaches the crew. He pulls up his sleeve, revealing a tattoo of the Time Pirates' insignia.

Dipper and Mabel gasp.

"C-C-Captain Time Beard!" says Blendin. "I've done as you asked. I searched through time and space to find the treasure buried by your previous captain, Grandfather Clock George. And I'll turn it over, just as we agreed!"

"*What?*" yell Dipper and Mabel in unison.

"You were working for the Time Pirates the whole time?" shouts Dipper.

"What about our cut of the treasure?" asks Mabel.

"HAR, HAR, HAR!" bellows Time Beard. A cuckoo pops out of a wooden clock below his mouth. "Let me tell you something, lass." He pushes the cuckoo back in and leans toward Mabel. "Your 'friend' here is the dumbest, most pathetic, worst time traveler in history. Naturally, he thought he could get respect if he joined up with the Time Pirates. So we told him the only way to prove his worth would be to find our lost treasure for us. And you fools helped him lead us right to it!"

"Hold on," says Dipper, turning to Blendin. "So you were just using us the whole time?"

"I'm s-sorry!" stammers Blendin, looking at Dipper and Mabel. "I'm just so tired of my mom calling me a loser.

Everyone knows Time Pirates are cool. But their selection process is very unfair and difficult and doesn't account for people with my body type! I had to try something desperate!"

"Like lying to us?" asks Mabel.

"Look, I'm really sorry," says Blendin. "Once I started the lie, it was hard to stop. I really had fun adventuring with you guys, though. I'll make sure the Time Pirates never rob you, honest!"

"Ho, ho, ho, kids, you've been plumb gullivered by this lunatic!" says Time Beard. "But the joke's on the lot of ye, because we would never, ever, in any time line let Blendin Blandin join our crew!"

"*What?*" screams Blendin. "But I went through all this work! And that tattoo really hurt!"

"You needed help from children to find the treasure! You're an embarrassment to the Time Pirates' Time Code of Time Conduct! But we'll be taking that treasure, thank you kindly," says Time Beard.

"How does it feel to be double-crossed?" asks Dipper, folding his arms.

Blendin holds his head in his hands. "Awww, jeez! I really Blendin-ed this up!"

Time Beard barks out a laugh. "Now, I imagine you children had a fun day of pirating and adventuring, but I recommend you go home and leave us this salty time dog so we can make him walk the time plank."

"All right," says Dipper.

"Wait, Dipper!" says Mabel. "I know Blendin's betrayed us, but he's still our friend! Kind of. Think of all the adventures we went on together!"

"Mabel, these Time Pirates are pretty scary and they're giving us a chance to save our own lives. That's a pretty good deal."

"Pfff, scary! That hasn't stopped us before!" says Mabel. "All day we've been taking on challenges and fighting enemies we thought impossible, and look how far we've come. What's a couple of pirates to a pair of time adventurers like us? We just have to make the right choice!"

Dipper thinks about it. "I dunno. The time plank sounds pretty awful."

Blendin gives the twins a pleading look. "I never meant to get you kids caught up in this!" he says. "Please, I know I don't deserve a second chance, but you're the only friends I've ever had! You've made so many right choices to get us here. Just make one more!"

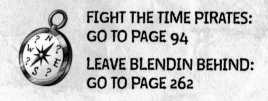

FIGHT THE TIME PIRATES:
GO TO PAGE 94

LEAVE BLENDIN BEHIND:
GO TO PAGE 262

SNEAK ABOARD THE TRAIN IN DISGUISE

Dipper steps across the line onto Blendin's side. "I know it's not as exciting," he says, "but I think we should put on some costumes, sneak aboard the train, and play it safe."

"BOOOOOOOOO!" says Mabel. "Boo, I say! BOO!"

"You're gonna get sick of booing me eventually," says Dipper.

Mabel smirks. "Will I?"

Fifteen minutes later, Mabel is still booing as they exit Granny Huggins's Present-Timey Costume Shop. When they emerge, they're wearing the perfect period garb to blend in on the train.

"I love this adorable bonnet!" says Mabel with a twirl, looking at her prairie attire in a storefront window.

Dipper wears a Stetson hat and a poncho that keeps snagging on cacti.

Blendin has squeezed into a hoop dress and petticoat.

At the train station, Dipper swipes train tickets from the pocket of a gentleman's unattended coat.

Blendin hands Mabel a laser blaster. "Just in case things get hairy," he whispers.

They board the train and take their seats.

Blendin fidgets. "As soon as this train leaves the station, we gotta find the Time Pirate who has the Time Key," says Blendin. "This corset is starting to damage my organs."

A well-to-do gentleman approaches Blendin. "Tell me, ma'am," he says, "is it warm in here or is it just your irresistible beauty?"

Blendin giggles.

The man sits down and continues talking to Blendin.

A whistle blows, and the train lurches forward out of the station.

Mabel whispers to Blendin, "Are you eddy-ray to go look for the ee-kay?"

"Go ahead without me. I want to see where this goes," says Blendin, gesturing to the wealthy suitor. Blendin fans himself, and the man orders a pair of sarsaparillas.

"Stupid Blendin, always getting rich gentleman callers," mutters Mabel. "It's not like I'm jealous or anything."

She and Dipper move from car to car toward the back of the train.

Eventually, they come across a sign between two rail-cars: ACCESS RESTRICTED BEYOND THIS POINT. PLEASE DO NOT ENTER.

"Well, this seems promising!" says Mabel. "There has to be something good back there if they're trying to keep people out. Maybe this is where the Time Pirate is hiding the Time Key!" She starts to push open the door.

A hand falls on her shoulder and spins her around.

"And who might you be?" asks a burly conductor.

Mabel stalls. "Uhhh. Uh . . . Uhhhhh . . ."

Dipper stalls, too. "Uh . . ."

What should they do, reader?

CONTINUE STALLING: GO TO PAGE 49

TAKE THE CONDUCTOR HOSTAGE: GO TO PAGE 138

SNEAK UP ON THE DRAGON FROM THE BACK

"**W**ell, I guess we should sneak up on the dragon from the back," says Blendin, shrugging. "If living with my mom has taught me anything, it's that you always want to sneak in the house through the back entrance to avoid getting yelled at!"

"These cliffs can't possibly be as scary as your weird home life!" says Mabel, beaming. "Let's go!"

Wind whipping through their hair, the group begins to scale the narrow, winding cliff side path, pressing their backs against the cold granite. They find the path is getting narrower and narrower, until it's only a few inches wide. Blendin makes the mistake of looking down and yelps when he sees they're a thousand feet in the air.

"See, this isn't so bad," says Mabel as she digs her nails into the stone wall. "We just have to make this experience into a fun game! Let's play I Spy!"

"Maybe we should focus on this climb," says Dipper.

"I spy something wooden and flutelike and falling away from me very fast," says Mabel.

"Is it the dragon flute?" asks Dipper.

"You bet it is!" says Mabel, grinning.

Dipper and Blendin groan.

"Great," says Dipper. "Now we're defenseless against the dragon!"

"We have three swords!" exclaims Mabel, thrusting her sword into the air. It slips from her hand and falls. "Two swords! I spy with my little eye something stabby and moving fast. . . ."

Dipper and Blendin groan again.

Within the hour, the gang has successfully looped around to the other side of the mountain, and they enter the cave. The walls are covered in ancient runes, and human skeletons and suits of armor line the dark, dusty corridors.

"Oh, man, I'm getting really creeped out by these skeletons, guys," says Blendin. "I've had a fear of skeletons ever since I got an X-ray and realized there's one hiding inside me at all times."

"Shhhh," says Dipper, cupping a hand to his ear. "What's that?"

A sound echoes through the cave.

"It sounds like . . . sobbing?" he says.

They round a corner and stop on the precipice overlooking a vast cavern. The cavern has an immense pile of gold in the middle. Resting on top, sprawled out and as large as a school bus, is a red dragon. The dragon appears to be sobbing. He blows his nose on the tattered tunic of a knight's skeleton.

Dipper, Mabel, and Blendin look at each other.

Suddenly, the dragon turns to face them. "WHAT?

WHO DARES DISTURB MY PRIVATE SOBBING TIME!" he yells in a booming Scottish accent. "YOU SHOULD GO!" He blows a ball of fire as a warning.

Dipper draws his sword. "This is it, guys! Get ready!" he yells. "We'll slay him for treasure and then dissect him for science!"

"Can we not dissect him?" shrieks Blendin. "What if he's got a skeleton inside?"

"Wait a minute, guys," says Mabel. "This dude's obviously going through some emotional biz right now. Maybe he just needs to talk it out. I'm a great negotiator! Remember that time I talked Grunkle Stan into wearing mascara for a whole day?"

"I don't know!" says Dipper. "Dragons are famously uncooperative!"

"If he's anything like my mom, he'll just throw candies at us!" shrieks Blendin. "*Hard* candies!"

"What should we do?" asks Dipper.

TALK TO THE DRAGON: GO TO PAGE 105
BATTLE THE DRAGON: GO TO PAGE 199

TRY TO JUMP OVER THE CHASM

"**If you won't throw me the rope,** I'll jump the chasm without one!" yells Dipper.

"*What?* That's crazy, Dipper! Don't do it!" screams Mabel.

Dipper clenches his fists. He walks a few steps back and then takes a running leap over the chasm . . . falling short of the edge by several feet and plummeting into the depths of the Infinitentiary.

"AAAAAH!" screams Dipper, his voice shrinking by the second.

He falls and falls for what feels like an eternity. Eventually, Dipper sees a maintenance sign hovering in the air next to him.

It reads:

**TIME TUNNEL'S TEMPORAL STATUS IS UNDER
CONSTRUCTION. YOU MAY EXPERIENCE A WAIT OF
UP TO INFINITY TO REACH THE OTHER SIDE.**

Suddenly, Dipper spies someone hovering next to him. "Chamillacles!" he says. "At least I'll have someone to talk to down here!"

"*Gleeee glor gleem glop glop!*" says Chamillacles.

"Oh, right," says Dipper.

Chamillacles begins to shed his skin.

Dipper shudders.

 THE END

THE SHORT AND FAT BLASTER

Dipper chooses the short and fat blaster.

"I've got a good feeling about this particular mystery death ray," he says, whirling it around his finger.

The sun is high in the sky.

The dry wind blows across the dusty street.

Dipper and Wild Eyes Joe begin their walk.

"One . . . two . . . three . . ." says Wild Eyes Joe.

Dipper wipes the sweat from his brow.

"Eleven . . . twelve . . . thirteen . . ." continues Wild Eyes Joe, whose spurs jangle with each step.

Dipper takes a deep breath.

"Fourteen . . . fourteen . . . What comes after fourteen? Aw, forget it. Eat lead!" shouts Wild Eyes Joe. He draws his weapon and shoots early.

Dipper ducks, wondering if he's already dead, but he realizes that Wild Eyes Joe missed. Smoke billows from a hole in Dipper's cowboy hat.

"*What?*" screams Wild Eyes Joe. "I never miss! Dangit, you're way too short for me to properly judge perspective at a distance. How far away are you, exactly?"

Dipper fumbles with his blaster. He pulls the trigger and—

WHOOOOOOOSH!

An enormous ball of glowing blue light surges from the tip of the blaster—straight into the dirt.

People in the town dive to the ground to shield themselves. Others run away from the sparking crater in the street. Shopkeeper Sprott flees his store in terror, screaming, "Hark! He is a destroyer of worlds! A smith of chaos! Runneth! Runneth if you can!"

Wild Eyes Joe's jaw drops, and his eyes go about as wild as his name would suggest. His weapon disintegrates in his hand. His lip trembles as he looks up at Dipper, then down at his singed chaps. He spins around and runs off with his bandit friends like a coward.

"Wait! Don't go!" Dipper yells to Wild Eyes Joe, handing off the blaster to Blendin. Dipper trips and nosedives into the crater.

"He's running away scared, Dipper!" says Mabel. "You won!"

"Yeah, but he has the Time Key we need!" says Dipper, standing and dusting himself off.

"Oh, yeah," says Mabel. "The Time Key. Totally forgot about that. What do we do now?"

Shopkeeper Sprott approaches them. "Well, I reckon it's time I come clean," he says. "I knew that convict there didn't have the key on account of I had it all along! I was just hoping I could convince y'all to scare him off so he'd quit hasslin' my customers and spittin' in my feed bags. And sure enough, you got rid of him, so here you go."

Shopkeeper Sprott presents Dipper, Mabel, and Blendin with the Time Key, which glistens like gold in the sunlight.

Mabel bites it. "Yup, it's a Time Key all right!" she says, beaming. "Now we can get the Time Pirates' Treasure!"

"This is awesome," says Dipper. "I mean, I don't feel great about being used, but thanks!"

"'Twas nothing. And on account of the good deed you've done, I'll forget I ever saw that witchcraft you committed," he says with a smile. "But don't push me." His smile fades. "Don't you dare. Push. Me."

"This is perfect, you guys," says Dipper. "You ready to finish our adventure and get that treasure?"

"I sure am!" says Blendin. "Let's ditch these dowdy outfits. I'm ready to trade in this cowboy hat for a crown." He sheds his hat and vest.

"And I'm ready to bedazzle both your faces with diamonds!" says Mabel, ditching her hat and vest, too.

Dipper shrugs. "Well, I don't want to be the only one dressed as a cowboy," he says, taking off his Old Western attire as well.

"Oooh, I'm so excited!" says Blendin. "My knees only shake this much when I think I'm going to be very rich very soon!" He motions to his jittering knees.

Mabel pokes one with a stick. It stops. She removes the stick and it starts shaking again. She does this several more times before Blendin knocks the stick from her hand.

Blendin produces the time tape from his jumpsuit and holds the Time Key firmly in his other hand.

The twins grab hold of the time tape together.

"Where we're going is very special," says Blendin. "It's not a time or a space but rather a place *between* time and space. Our lives flow on a river of time. And every choice we make is like traveling down a new, unique branch of that river. If you could see the fourth dimension, you could see the entirety of human history sprawled out like a river delta. Infinite lives and parallel universes coexisting. And now we're about to step out of the river—onto a secret hidden island wedged between the currents of time!"

"Oooh!" say Dipper and Mabel.

"I memorized that quote from a movie," says Blendin, beaming. "It was called *StellarCeption*, was forty-eight hours long, and was utterly incomprehensible. Very popular in time prison."

Blendin pulls out a measured length of time tape and lets go.

**TRAVEL TO THE TREASURE:
GO TO PAGE 145**

RIDE UP FROM THE OUTSIDE LIKE OUTLAWS

Dipper steps onto Mabel's side of the line. "Sorry, man, this just sounds like way more fun," he tells Blendin.

"Yeeee-haw! Ride 'em, cowboy! Bang-bang-bang!" says Mabel.

"I guess I can't argue with that," says Blendin, kicking the dust.

"Welcome to Loco Motive's, pardners!" shouts the shopkeeper as the three of them walk through the double doors of the robbery apparel store. "Your one-stop shop for thievin' supplies and robberphernalia!"

They look around. The shelves are stocked with weapons, bandanas, and white paint for covering wanted posters. A scorpion scuttles into a barrel labeled FAKE MUSTACHES and scuttles out wearing one.

"Give us three fast and strong horses with pretty hair!" yells Mabel.

The shopkeeper looks at her. "Do y'all have money or would you prefer to use our payment plan wherein you pay us from your future robberies?"

"Wait, you guys will let people buy supplies to commit robberies and pay you after the job is done?" asks Dipper. "Does anyone ever come back?"

"Not really," says the shopkeeper. "I reckon it's a flawed business model, but I'm not here to turn a profit. I'm here to serve the community!"

Blendin and Mabel each give an approving nod.

They dress up in bandanas and fake mustaches.

The shopkeeper leads Dipper, Mabel, and Blendin to a stable where three horses are waiting. Mabel grins. Blendin wipes the sweat from his brow.

WHOOOOOOOOO!

The exhilarating call of a train whistle rings through the air a moment later as Dipper, Mabel, and Blendin race on horseback across the open plains toward a speeding locomotive.

"HYAH, HYAH, giddyup, Black-Spirit-Beauty-Biscuit!" screams Mabel to her horse. She takes off her hat and waves it, letting the wind whip through her hair.

"Your sister is really taking to this with a frightening intensity," says Blendin.

"Yeah, she gets swept up in things sometimes," Dipper says with a shrug. "One time in third grade someone stole her pencil and she launched a mock police investigation to find it. She called it Bad Cop, Worse Cop and didn't stop until she got suspended for interrogating people."

"Let's just get in and get out," says Blendin. "We're intruding on the Calamity Brothers' turf, and trust me: we don't want to run into them!"

Dipper, Mabel, and Blendin close the distance and ride up alongside the train.

The engine driver spots them.

"My name's Mad Mabel Picante Pines and could you please stop this here train . . . or *else*!" yells Mabel.

"Or else what?" screams back the conductor.

"Or else I'll ask again, and this time, I won't say *please*," says Mabel, squinting.

Shrieking, the conductor throws some levers. The train starts picking up speed.

"Oh, no, guys! They're speeding up!" yells Blendin. "If we're gonna hop on this thing, we better do it now!"

Dipper makes a grab for the railcar but can barely hold on. "It's going too fast! Isn't there another option?" he asks.

Blendin points to a hole in the red rock cliffs ahead. "He's racing for that tunnel 'cause he knows we can't follow them inside!" he says. "If we took one of my laser blasters and shot the rocks above to block the entrance, then they'd have to stop!"

"Well, that's obviously the right choice!" yells Dipper over the rumble of the train.

"Not really! If we miss, we'll lose our chance to board, and by the time this thing charges up again, they'll be long gone. I guess what we need to know is . . . how good of a shot do you think you are? Especially while riding a horse?" asks Blendin.

Dipper thinks it over. "This is tough!" he says. "Should we risk our lives to hop aboard a fast-moving train? Or do I risk losing the train forever by taking the shot?"

"Just pick one, Dipper!" yells Mabel.

PERFORM A HIGH-SPEED BOARDING: GO TO PAGE 67

BLOCK THE PATH: GO TO PAGE 269

PLAY HIM IN CHESS

Dipper takes a breath. "I choose . . . chess!" he says.

"Yawn!" groans Mabel.

"Come on, Mabel," Dipper whispers. "This guy is a sword-swinging meathead. He's probably never seen a chessboard in his life! I'll beat him, and we get the key!"

The king calls Sir Swollsley into the royal gaming parlor.

Dipper cracks his knuckles and sits down at the board. "I'll go easy on you, buddy," Dipper says. "I'll let you be white and go first. Remember, pawns can move two spaces on openings, knights move in an L shape, and—"

"Oh, I am well aware," says Sir Swollsley as he removes his helmet, revealing that his face is adorned with multiple chess-themed tattoos. "I was the greatest chess player in mine fraternity!" He removes his breastplate. Winged chess pieces descend from stormy clouds and obliterate their enemies in a stunning mural tattooed across his chest. "NOW. WE. PLAY!" he bellows.

Dipper gulps and moves a pawn.

In four moves, Sir Swollsley checkmates him and throws up his fists in triumph. "Scholar's mate! WOOO!" yells Sir Swollsley. He points a finger in Dipper's face. "YES! The fair maiden is mine. In your face! In your dumb, weak child face!"

The king folds his arms across his chest.

Dipper bites his lip. "So . . . uh . . . okay, that did not go the way I expected. What if we, uh, tried one of those other challenges?" he asks.

The king only shakes his head and points at Dipper.

The knights drag Dipper, Mabel, and Blendin to the dungeon.

"No! You can't do this to us!" shouts Dipper.

"Yeah," says Mabel. "Who'll take care of Waddles?"

"Well, back to prison!" says Blendin. "I kind of missed it, honestly. Is that weird?"

For our heroes, this looks like . . .

 **THE END.**

MAKE A RUN FOR IT

"**W**ell, Mabel . . . there's only one choice left," says Dipper. He points the laser blaster. "Run! I'll cover us!"

The lawmen see the laser blaster and dive for cover.

"What in blazes?" one screams.

"He has some sort of pocket cannon!" screams another.

"Who—who are you?" asks the sheriff.

"Let the papers come up with a name!" shouts Mabel. "Yeee-haw!" She and Dipper flee on their horses.

Blendin runs after them and trips. Lawmen seize him.

Dipper digs his spurs into his steed, and he and Mabel ride off amid a storm of gun smoke. Across the dusty plain and past the creosote bushes, they speed into the red rock canyons surrounding the open plain.

"It looks like we've lost the lawmen," says Mabel.

"Yeah, but for how long?" asks Dipper.

✦ ✦✦ ✦

Days and nights pass as Dipper and Mabel continue their run from the law, eating berries by day and singing cowboy songs in the firelight by night. Dipper teaches himself to whittle. Mabel makes a sweater out of tumbleweeds.

Finally, their hunger gets the better of them, and they decide to sneak into town. On the way, they pass a stranger.

"Hi," says Dipper, "is this the road to Calamity Junction?"

The lonesome cowpoke takes one look at Dipper and

the color drains from his face. "Here, take my horse! Take whatever you want! Just don't hurt me!" he says.

The stranger runs into the hills.

"Hmmm, that was weird," mutters Dipper.

"Maybe this guy can help," says Mabel, turning to another passerby. "Hi, excuse me!"

The man drops his satchel and runs, shouting, "Aaah, it's them! The Calamity Brothers! RUN FOR YOUR LIVES!"

"Who? Where? What is going on here?" asks Mabel.

"Mabel, you won't believe it!" says Dipper. He points to a tree with a poster nailed to it. The poster features a drawing of the twins in their fake mustaches. The caption reads:

$10,000 REWARD FOR CAPTURE
MOST DANGEROUS VILLAINS IN THE WEST!

"Wait . . . the *Calamity Brothers*? Those famous outlaws Blendin told us about? They think that's us?" asks Mabel.

"Oh, no way!" exclaims Dipper. "Mabel, do you realize what's happened? We *are* the Calamity Brothers. They never existed on their own. The legend was about us all along!"

"Whoa!" whispers Mabel. "So what do we do now?"

Dipper scratches his chin. "I dunno. We already have a reputation. And a bunch of people just gave us free stuff 'cause they thought we were criminals. There's no way to get Blendin's treasure now. Wanna live out the rest of our lives as bandits? According to legend, we become millionaires!"

"Uh, *yeah*! That sounds amazing!" Mabel says, high-fiving Dipper. "Hey, look, there's another rube coming up the road!" says Mabel. "Let's go jack his stuff!"

"I call his spittoon!" yells Dipper as they ride off to shake down the stranger.

And so begins the rest of their lives as bandits: telling tales, going on adventures, walking a path of gold teeth and golden opportunities. The sunset is their home, the jackrabbits are their friends, and according to some folk songs, Mabel tames and learns how to ride a bear.

Though for them it's only the beginning,
dear reader, for you this is . . .

THE END.

SAY THEY'RE THE NEW ENTERTAINMENT

"**W**e're the new saloon entertainment!" says Dipper.

Wild Eyes Joe lets go of Dipper's collar and looks at him, Mabel, and Blendin. "Are you tryin' to tell me that you three are the Jumpin' Giddyup Gals?"

Dipper throws a sideways glance at Mabel and Blendin, who both shrug.

"Yes. Yes, we are," says Dipper.

Wild Eyes Joe gives Dipper a long once-over. "Well, all right, get on up there! We been waitin' f'rever!" he yells, grinning.

The whole saloon erupts into hooting and hollering.

Blendin and the twins stumble onto the stage.

"What do we do?" whispers Mabel to Dipper and Blendin. "Should I do my stand-up routine? I have a solid fifteen on scrunchies."

Wild Eyes Joe motions to a crate of instruments on the side of the stage.

Mabel picks up a tambourine.

Dipper grabs a cowbell.

Blendin picks up a banjo and, to everyone's surprise, plays a devastating lick.

The twins look at him, their mouths falling open.

"I spent a lot of time in prison! Learning to play the banjo kept the madness out!" Blendin says, tapping his head.

Dipper and Mabel shrug.

"Well . . . ah-one and ah-two and ah-three!" says Mabel. They start playing their instruments.

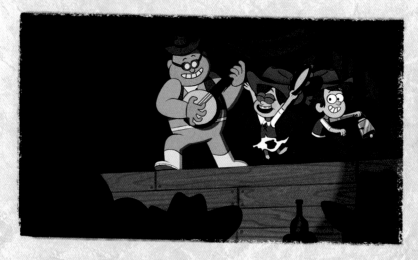

Mabel improvises a song:

Oh, we're traveling through the country,
And we're traveling back in time.
A mighty fine ol' treasure is what we aim to find.
But now we're playing music
For you scary folk!
Please, please, please, please don't hurt us.
Like everyone, we fear death!

"Seriously!" adds Blendin. "We're really, really, really afraid of dying!"

Blendin plucks out a sweet banjo finish and they all pose.

All the cowboys rise from their seats, scowling.

Mabel gulps. "Did we just enrage a room full of outlaws?"

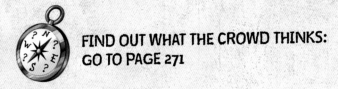

FIND OUT WHAT THE CROWD THINKS:
GO TO PAGE 271

WALK AWAY FROM THE ALTAR

Dipper looks at Mabel, holding the time tape, and then back at Wendinella. "I can't do it," he says. "You're everything I've ever wanted, Wendinella, but I belong in my own time! Where my friends and family are! And also running water and modern medicine!"

Dipper runs toward Mabel and Blendin.

A knight spots him and unsheathes his sword. "Halt!" he shouts.

Dipper jumps over the sword and tucks and rolls toward Mabel and Blendin. He grabs Mabel's ankle. "Pull the tape! PULL THE TAPE!" he yells. Mabel pulls the tape and *WHOOOSH*, the trio flashes back to present-day Gravity Falls. They head into the Mystery Shack.

"Well, it was a difficult choice, but it was the right choice," says Dipper, sighing. "Now I'm just gonna try not to think about it!"

Wendy walks into the Mystery Shack wearing a wedding dress.

"Hey, what's up, dude? Check out this creepy old dress I found!" she says.

Dipper chokes back tears and runs outside.

"Whoa, what's up with him?" she asks.

"Eh, we were just on this time adventure," Mabel explains, "and he had a chance to marry this girl who looked and acted exactly like you and he turned it down. I think he's really regretting it."

"Whoa, I have a time doppelganger?" asks Wendy.

"Yeah, it was really eerie. Her name was Wendinella!" says Mabel. "Blargghhh."

"Eww, gross," says Wendy.

"Tell me about it," says Mabel.

They sit there for a moment.

"Wanna use the time tape to go back in time and trade places with her, resulting in a series of wacky pranks and mix-ups?" asks Mabel.

"Absolutely!" says Wendy.

They team up with Blendin and pull the time tape.

To continue this story, please go out and buy the sequel to this book: *Mystery Twins: The Time Sisters' Quest for the Evil Time Twin.*

TAKE THE SHORTCUT

"**W**hy was I even asking?" screams Mabel. She pushes the racer to full throttle and speeds into the tunnel.

In almost complete darkness, Mabel navigates the twisting corridor before spilling back out into the light—a full racer's length ahead of *Racer T*.

The crowd goes wild.

Emperor Snorgshnog throws his opera glasses down in disgust.

The twins are back in the lead.

Toby speeds up alongside them, his racer within arm's reach of the twins'. He pulls a dagger from his sleeve and stabs it into the twins' unprotected fuel tank. "Stabby, stabby!" he cackles.

Mabel's control console lights up red.

"Dipper, we're losing fuel, fast! And we're almost at the finish line!" she yells.

Racer T maintains a steady lead as the twins slow down.

They radio Blendin. "Help us!" they shout.

"Ahhh, jeez, this is tough, you guys," says Blendin. "You've basically got two options. You can detonate your boosters and hope the blast pushes you over the finish line, but there's an equal chance it'll just send you careening into the wall."

"That sounds horrible!" screams Mabel. "What's our other option?"

"Well, there's a dip in the track coming up on your right," says Blendin. "If you steer into the pit, you might be able to slingshot yourself out and across the finish!"

"So, what's wrong with that?" asks Mabel.

"If your angle is even slightly off, you'll probably launch yourself into a time vortex, which . . . well, no one really knows what happens when you enter a time vortex!" says Blendin.

"Ah, man, these are some crummy choices," says Mabel. "And we have to choose quick."

"Which one is it gonna be?" Dipper asks her.

EXPLODE THE BOOSTERS: GO TO PAGE 10

JUMP THE JUMP: GO TO PAGE 243

THE LONG AND SKINNY BLASTER

Dipper chooses the long and skinny blaster.

"I hope this works," he whispers.

Dipper and Wild Eyes Joe meet at the dirt line.

Wild Eyes Joe scoffs at Dipper. "You call that a pistol?" He laughs, eyeing the weapon. "Looks like a silver lollipop! Which would be very valuable but *useless* in a shoot-out!"

Dipper narrows his eyes.

He and Wild Eyes Joe start to count paces.

"One . . . two . . . three . . ."

Dipper takes a deep breath.

"Ten . . . eleven . . . twelve . . ."

Mabel bites her nails.

Blendin bites Mabel's nails.

Mabel gives Blendin a creeped-out look.

"Twenty-eight . . . twenty-nine . . . DRAW!" says Wild Eyes Joe, with his weapon raised like a pro.

Dipper fires and—

WHOOOSH!

A giant blue ball of energy surges from Dipper's blaster and careens wildly through the street, leaving a jagged gash in midair that looks like a tear in the fabric of the sky.

"Uh, Blendin, was that supposed to happen?" asks Dipper.

Sparks shoot out of the gash, and a deep rumbling emanates from within.

"There was d-definitely something wrong with that blaster!" stammers Blendin, getting increasingly sweaty. "And b-by the looks of it, it ripped a hole in space-time!"

Mabel walks up to the rip in space-time and pokes it with a stick.

"Careful!" yells Blendin. "You don't want to risk opening it any further!"

"Oops," says Mabel. She's already torn an edge, and a flap of space-time hangs down limply like a loose poster corner. She tries to push it back up, but it just sags down again.

"Ah, jeez, this is not good!" says Blendin.

Energy explodes from the space-time rip and an assortment of creatures, humans, and machines from different eras begin to emerge. An enormous brontosaurus plods out of the rip and charges the horse corral. The horses panic and leap the fences, leaving their owners behind to be trampled. A Model T driven by Abraham Lincoln, with Jimi Hendrix riding shotgun, rolls out and starts doing donuts on the main street. Giant robot spiders from the future scurry out and start scaling buildings.

Everyone in the town screams and runs.

The gang huddles together.

"What do we do?" asks Mabel. "Abraham Lincoln is going to be really angry when he runs out of petrol!"

"The time schism won't stop growing!" says Blendin. "I really shouldn't buy time weapons on sale!"

The tear is growing ever larger as more and more creatures and beings from contradictory times pour out of it. The universe begins completely collapsing on itself.

Although it's supercool to look at, this means that for our heroes, their story has reached its . . .

 END.

NOT TO BE VENGEFUL

WHAT ARE YOU DOING HERE?

WHY ARE YOU WASTING TIME READING THIS PAGE?

You've been betrayed!

I'm the Omniscient Nameless Narrator, and even *I* want to kick that king's butt!

GO GET VENGEANCE!
RACE TO PAGE 41

ESCAPE IN THE MINE CART

"**There's no time to think!" yells Blendin.** He grabs the twins and tosses them into the rickety mine cart. "Let's get out of Time-Dodge," he says as he releases the brake lever.

The centuries-old mine cart shakes violently as it goes; it feels as though it's going to rip itself apart at every turn. Metal screeches and sparks fly as the iron wheels struggle to keep the cart on the track. The twins and Blendin duck as they sail under low-hanging stalactites and an overpass. Bones of dinosaurs flicker past them in the ancient strata of the walls.

"Guys, I think we lost him . . ." says Mabel. "So, uh,

should we maybe try to slow down now?" Her words are lost to the deafening *whoosh* of wind racing past the cart. She grabs the brake lever and tries to engage it, but it snaps off.

The mine cart picks up speed.

Dipper pulls out his flashlight. It flies out of his hand and disappears in the mine shaft.

They're in complete darkness.

They hold each other close just as—

SMASH!

The mine cart strikes a pair of bumpers and upends, throwing the gang forward. They scream but land softly in sand.

Blendin lights a match and makes an impromptu torch out of his cowboy vest. It looks like they're standing on a sandy beach in a cavernous chamber, beside a crystal-clear glowing blue pool.

Ahead of them is an enormous pair of oak doors and a sign that says TRESPASSERS BEWARE! A few glowing jewels are scattered on the underground beach.

Dipper says, "Everything about this feels very . . ."

"Pirate-y!" says Mabel with a smile.

"Guys. Beyond those doors!" says Dipper. "We must have found the Time Key!"

Blendin hops up and down with manic glee. "We did it! The treasure will be ours in no time! And we can finally stop making all these frustrating choices!"

Dipper, Mabel, and Blendin each put a hand on the doors.

Their fingers tremble, and they look at each other and grin.

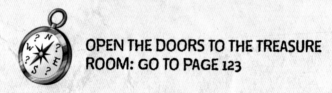 **OPEN THE DOORS TO THE TREASURE ROOM: GO TO PAGE 123**

CONFRONT THE DRAGON WITH THE FLUTE

"**W**ell, I guess we're going with confronting the dragon with the flute," says Blendin, shrugging.

"Perfect!" says Dipper, puffing out his chest like a knight. "Let's become legends or die trying."

"Yay! Death!" says Mabel.

They creep into the cavern, with Dipper leading the way with his torch.

Every crunch of human bones beneath their feet echoes off the craggy walls.

The dragon's breathing grows louder.

They round a corner.

There in front of them lies a winged, red-scaled dragon so massive its horns graze the top of the cave. The dragon slumbers atop a massive pile of treasure, which glints in the torchlight.

"Whoa, look at all this treasure!" says Blendin, running his fingers through it. "Forget the Time Pirates! We could grab this loot and live like kings!" He picks up a crown and puts it on his head. "Look at me, Mom! Who's unemployed and lacking confidence now?"

"Shhh," whispers Dipper. "You'll wake the dragon."

"You sound just like her!" says Blendin. "'Take out the time trash, Blendin! Stop using your stepdad's time deodorant, Blendin!' Well, this time, I'm in charge!" Blendin grabs an armful of gold coins. Under their weight, he tips over and lands with a *THUD* on his back. "Help!" he shrieks. "This armor is too heavy! I can't move!"

"Aw, he's like an upside-down turtle," says Mabel. "Look at his wiggling legs. Wiggle-wiggle!"

The dragon awakens with a start. "WHO GOES THERE?" he bellows in a booming Scottish accent, stretching out his long neck. "YOU ARE NOT WELCOME IN THE LAIR OF CONNERHEART THE DRAGON! YOU MUST GO!"

"Hurry!" yells Dipper. "Play the song, Mabel!"

Mabel blows into the dragon flute and plays the instrumental bridge from the Sev'ral Timez hit single "Cray-Cray."

"WHAT? WHAT IS THIS POPPY, MAINSTREAM THREE-CHORD TRASH?" the dragon fumes. "YOU THINK YOU CAN LURE ME TO SLEEP WITH THAT?"

"Mabel! Play something else!" shrieks Dipper.

"It's all I know!" says Mabel.

The dragon rubs his eyes, picks up a large bottle of neon blue mouthwash, swigs some and swishes it around a few times in his mouth, and then blows an enormous ball of flame.

WHOOOSH!

Well, it was worth a shot.

 THE END

THE FUTURE

"**The future!**" **exclaims Mabel.** "I want to buy a Hug-Bot! And see how extreme snack flavors become in a thousand years!"

"I don't know, Mabel," Dipper says. "The last time we went to the future, we were pitted to the death against time convicts and almost eaten by a thousand-foot baby."

"His name is *Time Baby*, for your information!" Blendin snaps. "And he rules humanity with a chubby, baby-soft fist! But he's not much worse than any other politician, honestly. Except for when he has his tantrums."

"Less yapping, more zapping!" says Mabel. "Let's go get that Time Key!"

Blendin takes out his time tape and pulls.

In an instant, the world around them warps into hyper-speed. Trees grow in fast motion. Clouds whip by in a blur. Cities rise and fall. Blendin's silly haircut flaps in the space-time breeze, then, suddenly—

THUD.

Dipper, Mabel, and Blendin land on a grungy street in the year 20705. The twins gaze around in wonder at the unrecognizable world. Buildings rise ominously into a perpetually dark sky as strange inhabitants whiz by using jetpacks and hover buggies. Time Baby's face is projected everywhere.

"Now, listen," says Blendin, donning a cloak. "The mission we're on isn't exactly sanctioned by the Time Anomaly Removal Crew, so we need to be in disguise. You should try to conceal yourselves."

Dipper turns his hat backward. Mabel pulls the collar of her sweater over her head. Blendin nods in approval and leads them down the street.

"Finding this key won't be easy," says Blendin. "Time Pirates are a ruthless and bloodthirsty bunch and would sooner be chrono-blasted than give up their secrets. They also wear really awesome hats and have cool catchphrases like 'shiver me time-bers' and 'clock the plank.'"

"You sure know a lot about Time Pirates," says Mabel. "If I didn't know any better, I'd think you wanted to be one!"

Blendin swivels around and turns bright red, stammering defensively. "M-me? Never! Those self-righteous watchbucklers are jerks with no regard for time laws! And they say really hurtful things sometimes!"

"Yikes, sore subject," mutters Mabel.

"Listen up," Blendin says. "The good news is two Time Pirates have been captured in this city: Davy Time-Jones, Scourge of the Seven Time Zones, and a madman known as Dos Hunthou. One of them might trade information about the key for his freedom. Then the treasure is ours!"

"A prison break!" exclaims Mabel. "Grunkle Stan's told us about those! Sounds fun!"

"Not exactly," says Blendin. "Davy Time-Jones is locked in the Infinitentiary, the most impenetrable prison of all time." Blendin gestures to a massive hovering complex shaped like a sideways figure eight. It swarms with security droids. "And Dos Hunthou has become an indentured servant to a wealthy space racer. In order to free him, we'd have to win a treacherous space race—which might sound fun, but moving quickly makes me dizzy and I have a fear of checkered flags. Plus, most of the racers die."

Dipper and Mabel look at each other.

What a difficult decision!

FUTURE PRISON BREAK: GO TO PAGE 13
SPACE RACE: GO TO PAGE 223

STAY FOR SARSAPARILLAS

"**All right, what the heck, I'll stay for *one*!**" says Mabel.

Dipper and Blendin groan.

Everyone on the train erupts in cheers.

Mabel sits down and has a sarsaparilla with the passengers while Dipper and Blendin each enjoy a sarsaparilla in the shadows. Dipper fidgets with his bandana while Mabel and the passengers laugh boisterously and tell stories. Soon one sarsaparilla turns to two, two turns to three, and then day turns to night.

By the time the sun has fully left the sky, the whole train has turned into a raucous party with Mabel at the head, leading the passengers in human wheelbarrow races, line dancing, and doing the limbo under tilling rakes.

Dipper and Blendin swallow the last swigs of their sarsaparillas and add their bottles to the pile of other empty ones surrounding Mabel.

Sometime around midnight, Mabel frees herself from the crowd.

"Sorry about that, guys," Mabel says to Dipper and Blendin. "But these Old West people sure know how to have a good time!"

The passengers stumble off the train.

"See ya, Larry!" says Mabel. "Later, Mad Dog! Way to be a limbo champion, Gold Dust Billy!"

A wild-eyed prospector jigs off the train and waves at her.

Dipper, Mabel, and Blendin stumble back to town . . . but something's wrong.

"Man, my stomach is doing a number on me," says Dipper.

"Mine, too," says Blendin. "And it can't be timesickness, otherwise I'd be coughing up miniature clocks."

"Yeah, I'm not exactly feeling so great, either," says Mabel. "What gives?"

Blendin pulls out a glowing electronic wand and scans Dipper's body.

The machine beeps and displays a data chart.

"Yup, there's your culprit!" he says, turning the screen for Dipper to see. "Dysentery! We all have dysentery. Probably shouldn't have ingested train-grade sarsaparilla."

"Oh, jeez!" says Mabel. "Is . . . is that bad?"

Dipper nods.

"This is horrible!" she says. "Are we gonna die?"

"Nah, not really," says Blendin. "We just have to go back to the present and take some medicine."

"Oh," says Mabel.

"Okay," says Dipper.

"Yeah, no biggie," says Blendin. He pulls the time tape and they zoom to the future.

As a group they see a doctor, and he cures them quickly. Although they are cured of dysentery, they all agree they are now literally SICK of time travel.

For our pals, it looks like . . .

 **THE END.**

SAY THEY'RE HERE TO PLAY CARDS

"**W**e're here for the game!" says Dipper.

Wild Eyes Joe leans closer to him and stares him square in the face. "Well . . ." he says, "why didn't you say so?" He laughs, letting go of Dipper's collar. "We love new players . . . because they always lose! Here, pull up a chair and ante up! We'll deal you in!"

Mabel and Blendin sigh in relief.

Dipper wipes the sweat from his brow. *That was close,* he thinks. "So what are we playing?" he asks. "Hold'em? Five-card stud? Aces high jackknife?"

Wild Eyes Joe laughs. "Ha-ha, will you listen to this kid?" he says. "Son, we don't play those childish games. There's only one game here serious enough for bloodthirsty desperadoes like us. It's called . . . *GO FISH.*"

"I've never played that one before! But I think I could get the hang of it," says Dipper, winking at Mabel and Blendin.

The outlaws scoff at Dipper and deal him in. They elbow each other, cackling.

An hour later, their smiles have all soured, because Dipper has won almost all their money.

Dipper rakes in the pile with a sheepish grin. "Beginner's luck, I guess!" he says. *I won't mention the hours and hours me and Mabel spent practicing go fish on the bus ride up to Gravity Falls,* he thinks.

"Son, what'd you say your name was again?" asks Wild Eyes Joe through gritted teeth.

"Uh . . . Dipper," he says.

"Dipper, huh. I don't know if I've ever heard of no outlaw named Dipper," says Wild Eyes Joe. "Mighty suspicious you've come around here, *Dipper*."

Dipper gulps. "That's, uh, pretty intimidating how you keep repeating my name like that." He feels everyone's eyes hone in on him.

The saloon gets quiet.

He, Mabel, and Blendin gulp.

Wild Eyes Joe stands up and walks over to Dipper. "You sure you've never played this before?"

"I mean, I think. Once or twice. Probably. Maybe?" Dipper says.

Wild Eyes Joe gives his friends a look. "Boys, I think we got a hustler at the table," he says.

They all stand up.

Wild Eyes Joe clamps a hand on Dipper's shoulder. "There's only two ways we settle situations like this, son. One's a shoot-out, and the other's a shoot-out. It's technically only one option, but I say it that way 'cause I think it sounds dramatic-like. So how about we go outside and settle this?"

Dipper turns and sees two outlaws restrain Mabel and Blendin by their arms.

The outlaws' gold teeth glint in the dusty light as they stare Dipper down.

Dipper feels in his pocket for something. Anything. He finds his flashlight. *Maybe I could use the flashlight to distract them*, he thinks.

What should Dipper do?

AGREE TO THE SHOOT-OUT WITH WILD EYES JOE: GO TO PAGE 120

DISTRACT THE OUTLAWS AND RUN: GO TO PAGE 73

BATTLE THE DRAGON

"**W**e can't risk it!" screams Blendin. "I think it's time for one of us to be brave and fight! I nominate Dipper!"

"*What?*" yells Dipper.

Blendin picks up Dipper and throws him onto the dragon.

"OFF! GET OFF ME, HUMAN!" yells the dragon, bucking.

Dipper grabs on to the dragon's shoulder and doesn't let go. He draws back his sword. "I guess I'm gonna slay you or something now! Sorry, man!" Dipper strikes the dragon—and watches his sword bounce off the scales.

The dragon cackles. "FOOLISH HUMAN! Your weapons are no use against my impenetrable scales! The only thing that can stop me is the sound produced by playing a DRAGON FLUTE!"

Dipper glares at Mabel.

"Sorry!" she says, shrinking down into her sweater.

Blendin slides down the rocks and approaches the dragon. "Hey, hey, Mr. Dragon! Please don't kill us! What if you gave us a riddle instead? Isn't that something dragons do?"

"Seriously?" groans the dragon. "Do I look like an idiot?"

"Hmm . . . This riddle is harder than I thought!" muses Blendin.

"EAT FLAMES!" roars the dragon. He takes a deep breath, charges up his fire breath, and . . .

FWOOOOOOSH!

**Looks like Blendin gave the wrong answer.
For our heroes, it's . . .**

 **THE END.**

ETERNAL YOUTH

"**E**ternal youth! Eternal youth!" shouts Mabel.

"IT IS DONE!" bellows the wizard, before handing Mabel a flask of glowing purple liquid.

Mabel pops the cork and holds it to the sky.

"Good-bye, wrinkles. Good-bye, crow's feet! Good-bye, weird cottage cheese spider skin that happens in your forties!" She toasts before gulping down the flask of youth serum. She burps and pounds her chest before handing the flask to Dipper. "Here you go, bro. Hit this."

Dipper swirls the liquid, looks at it cautiously, and then takes a sip. "Huh. How can we tell if it worked?"

Mabel shrugs.

Blendin guzzles the last of it. "Do I have any more hair?"

✦ ✦ ✦

In a few months, the twins and Blendin feel the same.

Dipper notices his scrapes and bruises heal quickly.

In a few years, Dipper and Mabel realize they're not hitting puberty like the rest of their classmates.

Blendin realizes he looks the same as always.

In a few decades, everyone they've ever loved has perished in the Time Baby uprising.

"I'm starting to think this was a bum deal, guys," says Dipper a long time later. "It's been thousands of years and my voice still hasn't dropped."

"Yeah, and I'm finally starting to run out of new sweaters to wear," says Mabel. "This is a real bummer."

"Do I look any younger?" asks Blendin.

"You look . . . older," says Mabel. "Poor guy."

"What should we do with our free time?" asks Dipper.

"Let's dance in style, let's dance for a while," Blendin says.

"All we have is our boxes of stuff from throughout history," mutters Mabel. "Hey! Maybe we should open a Museum of the Past!"

"Ooooh! I like museums! And this will keep our minds off of the existential horror of being immortal!" says Dipper.

So the twins get to work making their museum, which is actually very educational and popular in the future.

Blendin eternally mops the floors.

But the search for the treasure has reached its . . .

 **END.**

STEAL A SPACESHIP

"**L**et's steal a spaceship!" yells Mabel. "I've made a lot of paper airplanes, so I think I know a little something about piloting." She runs down the hall and toward the hangar.

The sound of running Infinitentiary guards fills the air, growing louder.

Dipper, Blendin, Davy Time-Jones, and Chamillacles bolt after Mabel.

Inside the hangar, they pile into the first available ship. The moment the doors close, they hear laser blasts from the guards' weapons ricocheting off the sides of the spacecraft.

Mabel takes the captain's chair and fires up the engines. "Dipper, you're on lasers!" she barks. "Davy, you're my first mate!"

"Yarrrrgh," says Davy Time-Jones, pumping his fist.

"Chamillacles, just sit next to me, make alien grunts, and wear a bandolier," says Mabel. "Trust me, you'll be a fan favorite."

"Oooh, oooh, what about me?" asks Blendin.

"You, don't touch anything!" yells Mabel.

"This seems like a lot of responsibility," Blendin says, sweating.

The spacecraft rocks under the impact of the laser blasts.

Mabel hits some switches and it lifts, throwing everyone off balance.

The guards scramble to close the giant doors in front of the craft.

Mabel hits the thrusters, and they speed off into outer space. "WOO-HOO!" she screams as she executes a g-force-inducing barrel roll. "Wow, being a hotshot rogue pilot is easy! You just need to have no idea what you're doing!"

Blendin, Dipper, and Davy Time-Jones catch their breath.

Red warning lights flash overhead.

Chamillacles makes babbling noises.

"He says 'incoming'!" says Davy Time-Jones, pointing out the window.

Their flight path is blocked by an enormous looming spaceship the size of the Infinitentiary.

Mabel turns on the ship's communication screen, which is signaling an incoming video call.

The screen flickers on, revealing a lobster-headed humanoid. "STOP, CONVICTS! STOP FLEEING AT ONCE!" he says. "I AM GENERAL CRUSTACEOUS LOB-STAR! WE HAVE YOUR PATH COMPLETELY BLOCKED!" He clacks his lobster claws.

Mabel looks away from the screen. "It's true!" she shouts. "What should we do?"

Davy Time-Jones scans the horizon. "There's only two ways we can escape!" he says. "One, we fly through that craggy, dangerous asteroid field over there!" He points to a massive asteroid field.

"Are you crazy, man?" yells Blendin. "That's impossible to navigate through! Also, our ship is being piloted by an oxygen-deprived twelve-year-old girl!"

"The odds are a million to one!" says Dipper.

"Never tell me the odds," growls Mabel, "because I'm super bad at math."

"What's option number two?" asks Dipper.

"We fly back at 'em head-on and get past them before they can turn that hulking ship around!" shouts Davy Time-Jones.

"But that's crazy! That's flying directly into danger!" yells Blendin.

"*GLEEP GLORP!*" squeals Chamillacles, beating his chest.

"Watch your language!" shouts Blendin.

"It's up to the captain to decide!" says Davy Time-Jones, turning to Mabel.

Mabel stares out the window and gulps.

FLY PAST THE GIANT SHIP: GO TO PAGE 60

FLY INTO THE ASTEROID FIELD: GO TO PAGE 52

SURRENDER

Dipper reactivates the laser blaster and puts his finger on the trigger.

Mabel sighs. "Dipper, wait! What are we gonna do, spend the rest of our lives as outlaws?" she asks.

Dipper scratches his chin. "I'm open to it," he says. "I've always wanted to learn how to whittle."

Mabel shakes her head. "We should turn ourselves in. It's the right thing to do," she says. "Also, riding a horse hurts my butt."

"Aw, all right," says Dipper. He powers down the blaster.

With heavy sighs, Dipper and Mabel put up their hands and walk outside.

The sheriff and his crew pounce and cuff the twins, taking Dipper's laser blaster.

"Well, hooooey! Looks like we caught ourselves a pair of regular old bandits," says the sheriff while dancing a jig and slapping his spurs. "You two have caused a *lot* of problems. Looks like y'all are gonna be in jail for a looooong time. Throw 'em in the wagon!"

The lawmen throw them in the back of a stagecoach and drive it toward town.

Dipper and Mabel shimmy toward the front, where the sheriff sits and whittles casually.

"So, uh, Mr. Sheriff, what's the punishment for what we did?" asks Mabel.

"Train-nappin'?" he asks. "Well, if it were up to me, I'd make y'all dress up like little trains and walk through town, and when someone tried to rob you, I wouldn't stop them. See how you like it. But I'm a touch odd in the head, so they don't let me choose punishments no more."

"Well, who does decide the punishments?" asks Dipper.

"Judge Hangamanforanycrime," says the sheriff. "And I warn you, he lives up to his name. He is indeed an actual judge."

Dipper and Mabel tremble.

"He's only let a criminal off once," says the sheriff, "and it was on account of him being a child!"

"But *we're* children!" shouts Dipper.

"What, you two bloodthirsty ne'er-do-wells?" The sheriff laughs. "You're clearly adults who are just short on account of the malnutrition that's so popular in these times."

"It's true!" yells Mabel. "Look long and hard at my brother here!"

The sheriff squints at Dipper. "Well, I'll be hoodwinked. You *are* children! Hmmmm . . ." He pulls out a key and unlocks them. "I reckon the townsfolk of Calamity Junction wouldn't get much satisfaction out of usin' capital punishment on children. How about we let this go and, say, give you a second chance?"

"Really? Is there a catch?" asks Dipper.

"The catch is do it before I change my mind!" says the sheriff.

Dipper and Mabel spring to their feet.

"Thank you so much, and we are soooo sorry," says Dipper.

"Seriously, so, so sorry!" says Mabel, dusting herself off.

"And take this weird shiny spoon back!" shouts the sheriff, tossing Dipper his laser blaster.

The twins race the short distance into town and stop inside the general store.

"Well, now that we've got out of that all right, what should we do next?" asks Mabel.

Blendin stumbles into the store, dusting off his pants and grumbling. "Well, I'll tell you what you *shouldn't* do, and that's try to seduce a wealthy businessman out of his riches. The moment my wig fell off he kicked me out of a moving train! These bruises will heal fine, but my pride . . ." He stares off into the distance.

"I'm just gonna try to forget I heard all that," says Dipper. "Looks like we should explore one of those other options if we're ever going to find this key."

"All right, we're going to need to look the part again," says Blendin.

Dipper returns the laser blaster to Blendin and throws on a cowboy hat and boots. Mabel and Blendin follow suit.

In their new disguises, they step outside.

CONFRONT THE OUTLAWS IN THE SALOON:
GO TO PAGE 237

EMBARK ON A MINING ADVENTURE:
GO TO PAGE 255

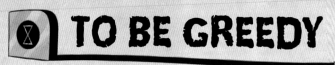

TO BE GREEDY

"**Y**ou know what?** I can answer my own question," says Mabel. "Let's get double rich!"

Dipper shrugs and high-fives her. "So what do we do?" he asks.

"Well, we time-jump back," says Blendin, "to right before the Time Pirates ran away. We take over their time ship and lives. Then we live a salty life of danger, robbing and looting throughout all time!"

"Sounds good to me!" say the twins as everyone joins hands.

Blendin pulls the time tape. But something's wrong. The time tape is sparking and hissing, and what's normally a flash of blue light is red.

After a particularly painful time jump, Blendin and the twins land in a reddish-black desert with strange misty black clouds stretching as far as the eye can see. Foggy muttering figures that are hard to make out stumble around like zombies in the distance.

"What happened? Where are we?" yells Mabel.

"Oh, jeez," says Blendin. "I forgot that because we were on a time island, out of time sync with any time stream, we couldn't jump or it would dump us in an inescapable time pocket."

"A WHAT?" screams Dipper.

"Yeah, I am starting to really regret getting greedy back

there. There's almost a lesson in this . . ." says Blendin.

Mabel runs up to one of the shadowy figures. "Excuse me, sir or madam, do you know a way out of this purgatory biz?"

The figure looks up beneath a mop of brown hair. It's Mabel.

"Page fifty-four," says the strange lifeless Mabel double. "I'm looking for page fifty-four."

"Page thirty-two . . ." moans another one. "I have to turn to page thirty-two."

Dipper and Mabel start grabbing the shadowy figures and turning them around, only to discover that all of them are gaunt, weary clones of *themselves*.

They see themselves in cowboy outfits, in prison uniforms, versions of themselves from every path of their adventures that ever went wrong.

"Ahhh, what is this place?" asks Dipper.

"It's worse than I thought," says Blendin. "We're in the Land of Malfunctioning Time Lines. In countless universes, you guys went on this journey with me today. A handful of them, probably twelve million, ended in death or getting lost in the time stream or just failing all around. For whatever reason, all those loose time ends gravitate together through the time-verse and wind up here. Like burnt potato chips at the bottom of the bag."

"You have to get us out of here!" yells Mabel.

Twenty feet away, a different Mabel yells the same thing at a different Blendin.

"Whoof, this didn't turn out great!" says Blendin. "It's almost like we've reached the . . ."

"WORST POSSIBLE ENDING," mutter millions of dreary clones in unison.

"Help!" yells Dipper. "Someone help us!"

His voice is lost in the din of thirty-six million desperate wandering souls.

 THE END

PRETEND TO CARE ABOUT MORALITY

"**Sorry, I gotta pause** and think about the ethics of this!" Mabel yells over the din of the engine. "I'll look really bad if I don't at least consider it!"

She eases off the throttle and slows down as she approaches the shortcut.

"Hmmmmmmmmmmmmmmmmmmmmmmmmmmmmm-mmmmmmmmmmmmmmmmmmmmmmmmmmmmmmmmmm-mmmmmmmmmmmmmmmmmmmmmmmmmmmmmmmmmm-mmmmmmmmmmmmmmm," she says. "Okay, let's do it!"

TAKE THE SHORTCUT:
GO TO PAGE 178

FIND THE MISSING WIZARD IN THE DUNGEON

The trio huddles and whispers. Then they turn back to the king.

"We chose searching the dungeon!" says Dipper. "Whatever the danger, we three heroes are prepared to do what it takes!"

"I think we'd all like to meet a wizard," says Mabel. "They always have silly names and neat things in their pockets."

"So be it!" says the king. "Guards, show them the entrance to the Labyrinth of Unfathomable Horrors!"

"Wait, hold up," says Dipper. "Say that name again?"

"The Labyrinth of Unfathomable Horrors!" repeats the king, grinning. "It is five hundred miles of twisted corridors full of traps and dead ends designed to make all who enter them go completely mad! That's why the wizard chose to hide down there. He knew no one would be stupid enough to follow him inside!"

The twins and Blendin look at each other, their eyes wide.

"On second thought, maybe we'll just do one of the other quests," says Dipper. "Didn't you say something about two other opt—"

"I tire of this conversation!" squeals the king, pounding his scepter down. "My mouth is not for debating! It is for being fed kingly delights! Guards, take them away! And feed me something on a stick so I don't have to move!"

The knights drag the gang out of the throne room and lead them down a dank spiral stairwell that runs deep below the castle. It grows increasingly dark and cobweb-infested as they descend the twisting stairs. They shudder in the cold as their shaky footsteps echo in the freezing air.

"I sure am glad I'm wearing a sweater right now," says Mabel. "Come to think of it, this is the first time all summer it's been appropriate."

The group approaches two massive oak doors secured by an enormous crossbeam. Three knights struggle to lift it. Wails of suffering sound from behind the doors.

The knights hand Dipper a flickering torch as they shove the trio through the double doors and into the darkness beyond.

"So, this wizard character. Where can we find him?" Mabel asks the knights. "Got any hints? Maybe one of those keychain beepers that helps you find your wizard in a large parking lot? Beep-beep?"

The knights slam the doors in their faces.

"Rude!" Mabel calls out.

Dipper holds up his torch, revealing an arched hallway stretching for what seems like an endless distance ahead of them. The floor is dust. The walls are made of moldy bricks and bones. A barely legible message scrawled on the wall reads:

THERE IS NO BATHROOM HERE

They all shudder.

"Well, I guess there's only one way to go," says Dipper.

"You know, this all might seem bad," says Blendin, "but it's actually quite impressive when you remember that this was built by human hands, centuries before modern tools and—"

"Ah-ah!" says Mabel, holding a finger to his mouth. "Now is quiet time."

The group hears an eerie moan of pain echoing down the dark hallway.

"Ah! A g-g-g-generally unpleasant noise!" stammers Blendin, hiding behind the twins.

"It sounds like a walrus giving birth to a camel," says Mabel.

"Well, the only direction we can move is toward it," says Dipper.

He, Mabel, and Blendin continue creeping toward the moaning until they see, hunched in the shadows, the bony silhouette of a skeletal form ravenously gnawing the head off a fish.

Dipper steps toward it, lifts the torch, and screams when he sees . . .

"Toby DETERMINED?" Mabel shouts.

Sure enough, it's their hometown reporter and failed tap dancer, Toby Determined. "Oh, hey, friends!" he says, offering them the chewed remains of his fish. "Want some cave fish? It's blind, so it doesn't know it's being eaten alive!"

"What are you doing in here?" asks Dipper. "How is this even possible?"

"Well, it's a funny story!" says Toby. "I was eating a microwavable dinner-for-one while trying to get mayo stains out of my favorite pair of sweatpants—"

"This is literally the saddest story I've ever heard," says Mabel.

"—when I was suddenly hit by a glowing purple time portal and wound up here!" continues Toby. "Apparently, the townsfolk thought I was some kind of 'sadness troll' and locked me in this dungeon for the last year! There's all sorts of fellas down here. I even saw a wizard once."

"Ah, jeez, s-sorry about that," stammers Blendin. "There's an eensy-weensy chance that that futuristic time blast *might* have been my fault."

"No, it's been great here!" says Toby. "I've made friends with a rat, and these dungeon rags are the cleanest clothes I've ever worn! Treat yourself to a sniff!"

"Not happening," says Dipper.

"Well, hey, if you know your way around here, maybe you could help us!" says Mabel with a smile.

"One second, group meeting," says Dipper. He pulls Mabel and Blendin aside. "Mabel, what are you doing? Do you really wanna spend the next six hours walking in complete darkness with Toby 'Have Some Cave Fish' Determined?"

"Aw, come on, Dipper, he isn't that bad," she says. "If you cover his face with your thumb, you don't have to look at it. Besides, he might help us find the wizard!"

Dipper thinks about it long and hard.

FOLLOW TOBY THROUGH THE DUNGEON: GO TO PAGE 141

TURN DOWN TOBY'S OFFER AND LEAVE HIM: GO TO PAGE 136

MEDIEVAL TIMES

"**L**et's pick medieval England!" says Mabel.

"I agree!" says Dipper. "Castles! Treasure! Wizards!"

"And free pigs just wandering in the street. IN THE STREET!" squeals Mabel.

"Yeah, plus if their paintings are any indication, I feel my body type was way more appreciated in those days," mumbles Blendin. "Let's go find that Time Key!"

Blendin pulls the tape.

Dipper and Mabel put their hands on his shoulders before—

WHOOOOSHHHH!

Blurring lights swirl about, followed by a static pop as they travel through space and time and—

SPLASH!

—land in a pool of mud in the middle of a feudal hamlet. Countless busy villagers freeze in stunned silence and gaze upon the trio.

"This is really awkward," says Dipper.

"Yeah," says Mabel. "It's like that time I called a boy I'd never met by his name because I looked it up online like a creep."

The rush of horse hooves shatters the peaceful silence, and a band of elegantly armored knights rides up.

"Whoa, shiny knights! Are you here to take us to our destinies?" asks Mabel.

"No," says the lead knight with a flip of his visor. "We're here to take you to the king!"

"The *hot* king?" asks Mabel.

"No. The tyrannical dictator king," says the knight.

"But on a scale from hot to not, how would you rate him?" she asks.

They all stare at each other uncomfortably for a moment.

The gang is stripped of their weapons. They are led into a stately throne room and thrown on the hard, cold cobblestone floor. Before them sits a pot-bellied king with a long white beard. He eats fanciful foods and giggles to himself. He speaks in a high nasal register. "Tell me, what brings you wretched lot to my kingdom?"

Dipper stands up and opens his mouth but he has his legs kicked out from beneath him.

"Kneel when you address the king," grunts a tall knight.

Dipper coughs. "Sorry, Your Majesty, we meant no disrespect," he says. "We've come to your land in search of a key. Just a plain old key. We mean only to find it and not get in your way. At all. Or anything. True story."

The king strokes his regal beard. "A key, you say? Could you describe this . . . key?"

Dipper and Mabel look at Blendin.

"Y-yes, Your King," says Blendin. "It belongs to a group of feared and respected pirates led by a man with clocks in his beard."

The king trembles. "Shiver me in my deepest of timbers, I know one of these pirates you speak of! He left a key here and told me not to tell anyone about it!"

"He did?" Dipper, Mabel, and Blendin say in unison.

"Furthermore, I'd be happy to tell you more about it," says the king.

"You would?" asks Dipper. He almost stands, but when the tall knight moves toward him, he kneels back down. "That's great," he says, "and disconcertingly straight-forward. . . . Usually we have to—"

"I will tell you if you complete one of *three* royal tasks for me!" says the king.

Dipper, Mabel, and Blendin sigh.

"I knew it was too good to be true," mutters Dipper. "All right, King, what do you need?"

"Task the first!" shouts the king. "My daughter is being courted by a knightly suitor!"

"You go, girlfriend!" says Mabel.

"Alas," says the king, "the suitor is an honorless brute. He's very annoying, and I'd hate to have him around my kingdom more than he already is. If you can defeat him in a contest of valor and rid me of him, my information will be yours!"

Dipper gulps.

"Task the second!" yells the king. "A dragon has stolen my fanciest goblet and is covetously hoarding it! It would benefit me greatly if you can slay him and bring it back!"

"Oh, pick the dragon, pick the dragon!" chants Mabel. "But we're not slaying it," she whispers.

"Task the third!" shouts the king. "My best wizard has gone mad and hidden away in the dungeon. I need someone to go into the catacombs to find him and bring him back to me! Can you help me?"

BATTLE THE KNIGHT: GO TO PAGE 229

SLAY THE DRAGON: GO TO PAGE 6

FIND THE MISSING WIZARD IN THE DUNGEON: GO TO PAGE 214

SPACE RACE

"**A** space race!" shout the twins, high-fiving.

"Blendin," says Dipper, "what exactly is a space race again?"

"A space race is a very thrilling, very dangerous sporting event, similar to what people in your time call a chariot race," says Blendin. "Racers ride in a titanium pod pulled by two turbine pods on cables, and they race their pods through canyons and deserts to see whose pod goes the fastest! We call it the Zoom-Zoom Bleep Blop Fun-Fun Derby."

The twins stare at Blendin.

"Everything here is named by Time Baby," says Blendin.

"So where do we get a space racer?" asks Dipper.

"Well . . . they're very expensive and I don't know if I can afford to lose that money," says Blendin. "I've been saving up my space credits to buy a large pillow to drown out my mom's constant criticisms."

"Pillow shmillow!" shouts Mabel. "If we free Dos Hunthou and get the Time Key to unlock the Time Pirates' Treasure, you can buy one hundred pillows. Or even a new mom!"

"A new mom . . ." mutters Blendin, clearly considering it.

"Besides, we've played tons of racing video games," says Dipper, shrugging. "Driving one of these is probably just like that!"

"Well, okay," says Blendin. "I know a place that sells 'em discounted."

He leads the twins into a seedy-looking junkyard on the outskirts of the city. Blendin removes his cloak as the hot sun blares down on them in the dusty air.

Signs hanging from a barbed-wire fence warn BEWARE THE TIME DOGS and TRESPASSERS WILL BE SENT DOWN UNDESIRABLE TIME LINES.

In an open garage is a titanium space racer.

Dipper runs his hand along its gigantic engine. "I wonder how fast this goes . . ."

"Over five hundred time miles per time hour per parsec," comes a voice with a congenial southern accent.

A balding, legless cyborg wearing a bright Hawaiian shirt glides out of the small trailer in the lot's corner on a hovering platform. "Yup, this space racer here is a real beauty or my name ain't Glorglax Gleeful!" says the cyborg. "My family's been selling space racers for low, low prices since the dark ages: 1970! You fellas looking to enter a space race?"

"Dos Hunthou," says Blendin, holding up a tattered WANTED poster with a picture of the former Time Pirate. "We want to win this servant's freedom in the next race."

"He has a fancy key we want for magic reasons!" says Mabel.

Glorglax Gleeful eyes Mabel up and down before spitting into a hovering spittoon. "Now this here is the finest space racer in all of 20705. It's practically *guaranteed* to win you that race. So as a smart customer like yourself can assume, it won't be cheap."

"How much?" asks Dipper.

"I'll cut you a deal and give it to you for thirty thousand credits," says Glorglax.

"We'll take it!" says Mabel. She extends her hand to shake on it.

"*PTHBBBBBB!*" Blendin spits out his time lemonade. "WHAT? That's more than my entire life savings!" he screams. "I only have twenty-one thousand credits! And three pennies I dug out of a bird feeder! And that's everything!"

Glorglax rubs his chin and looks Blendin up and down. "Well, now," he says, "lemme see if there's something I can do. I'm a sporting sales-borg, and, well, I can see y'all need this, so how about this: I've got another racer I can sell you for twenty-one thousand credits. It's not guaranteed to win any races, but it'll do."

Glorglax ponders for a moment.

"Buuuuuut to tell you the truth, I'd really like to see you

in this beauty," says Glorglax. He pats the more expensive space racer. "So here's what I propose. In my pocket is a little thing called a probability square." He produces a small wooden cube colored red on three sides and blue on the rest. "How about we roll it, and if it comes up red, I'll let you have this racer for twenty-one thousand credits?"

"Wait, what happens if it comes up blue?" asks Mabel, peering at him.

"Well, I can't say I haven't been eyeing your adult friend here and his doughy but sturdy lifting arms," says Glorglax. "I reckon I'd take him on as my indentured servant if y'all lose."

Blendin gasps. *"What?"* he says.

"Fine," say Dipper and Mabel.

Blendin gawks at them. "I can't risk being an indentured servant!" he says. "I really hate doing things, particularly doing things all the time!"

Mabel sighs. "I dunno," she says. "Maybe we can make do with the cruddy space racer and not risk it."

ROLL THE PROBABILITY SQUARE: GO TO PAGE 47

BUY THE LESSER RACER: GO TO PAGE 265

MAKE A RUN FOR IT

The lawmen storm into the train car.

"Well, Mabel . . . there's only one choice left," says Dipper. He points the laser blaster at the roof of the railcar and fires. There's an enormous flash of bright light and a deafening boom that blows out all the train windows.

The lawmen dive for cover.

"What in blazes?" one screams.

"He has some sort of pocket cannon!" screams another.

"Who—who are you?" asks the sheriff.

The train lurches forward and begins to pick up speed.

Dipper quickly grabs Mabel by the arm and runs out the opposite side of the train, leaping from the shattered railcar window.

The twins hit the ground, roll, stand, and run.

Blendin stumbles out the door of the train and rolls toward them, hitting a patch of cacti along the way.

The twins wave good-bye to the lawmen as the train chugs by.

Blendin walks toward the train tracks.

"Woo-hoo!" says Mabel. "Best day ever!"

"Yeah!" says Dipper. "Close call!"

"Oh, no!" shouts Blendin, lifting his crushed time tape from the tracks.

They look around. There's only desert for miles.

"Uh . . . now what do we do?" asks Dipper.

"Oh! Birds! And puppies!" says Mabel, smiling.

"Mabel, those are vultures . . . and coyotes," says Dipper.

It looks like our heroes have reached . . .

 THE END.

BATTLE THE KNIGHT

"**That knight is going down!**" **says Dipper.** "For the honor of the kingdom!"

"And to get that sweet treasure!" whispers Blendin.

Dipper elbows him in the gut.

The king twiddles his fingers and grins. "Oh, goody-good-good, I was hoping you would choose this task!" he says. "Come. Follow me. You must meet him!"

Dipper, Mabel, and Blendin follow the king down dim, stony hallways. The knights follow behind them, prodding at their heels with long spears.

Mabel whispers to Dipper. "Pssst. Are you sure about this? You don't usually handle competitions well. . . ."

"Come on, Mabel," says Dipper. "We're in medieval England. If worse comes to worst, I can just dazzle this guy with our future technology, like calculators and shoelaces. Then we'll just find the Time Key and run! Hopefully the king will tell us about it after we complete his task."

They round a corner and step out onto a carved stone balcony overlooking a courtyard. Below, knights and squires practice their swordsmanship. Each has his head down and walks hunched over, except for one beefy knight standing in the center with his chest out and chin up, smiling and screaming. The king motions toward him.

"THIS IS MY HOUSE! Come at thee! Come at thee, bro!" says the knight. "Look at this armor! Do you know how much this armor cost?" The knight shoves a squire's face into his silver breastplate.

"Well, I can see why you don't want him around," Dipper tells the king.

The king clears his throat. "Ahem. Sir Swollsley!" he calls to the knight. "There's another suitor here to challenge you for the fair maiden's hand!"

"Send down the suitor, bro," yells Swollsley. "Let me vanquish him so I can marry down with your sweet, sweet daughter and get all up in that kingdom. Verily, bro."

"Yes, yes, I'll send him down," says the king. He flashes a false smile to the knight before whispering to Dipper, "You better win this, boy."

"Now a contestant must decide betwixt two challenges," says the knight. "One of wits, such as chess, and one of brute strength, such as jousting. Tell me, kid, which do you choose?"

PLAY HIM IN CHESS: GO TO PAGE 168

JOUST AGAINST HIM: GO TO PAGE 19

TRUST THE PROSPECTOR

"**W**e're gonna trust you, Jugsley," Mabel tells the prospector.

"Are you sure about this?" whispers Dipper. "This guy seems two strings short of a banjo."

"Come on," says Mabel, motioning to Jugsley. "That's what we thought about McGucket, and he turned out all right in the end. Besides, no one is so crazy that they'd look you in the eye and deliberately lead you to your death!"

The twins and Blendin follow Jugsley a few steps down the path.

"Welp, here's your deaths!" says Jugsley. He cheerfully kicks Blendin and the twins into the pit. "Whooo-eeee, you lot fell for that right quick!" He laughs. "Wow, that was a dumb choice! I'm so clearly a maniac!"

Mabel spits out coal dust. "Let us out of here, you monster!"

"Sorry, but I reckon I can't let y'all be sneakin' around my boron mines trying to steal my precious boron," says Jugsley. He starts nailing boards over the top of the pit. "In twenty-odd years we're gonna be at war with the Australians and we're gonna need all the boron we can get. Don't believe me? Sniff some boron dust like I do every morning and it'll start makin' sense right quick!" He continues sealing the pit.

Dipper glares at Mabel. "What was that you said about never making the obvious choice?" he asks her.

Mabel slugs Dipper in the shoulder as Jugsley cackles. They sit in silence in the pit . . . forever.

At least they have boron.

 **THE END**

FLY THROUGH THE SHIP

"**W**e're going in!" shouts Mabel. She jerks the controls and steers their spaceship toward a wide open exhaust port on the front of the massive spacecraft before them.

A fleet of fighter crafts speeds toward them, but Dipper quickly neutralizes them with the onboard laser gun. "Finally, all the time I've spent watching sci-fi movies instead of making friends is paying off!" he exclaims.

Mabel steers their craft toward the opening and threads the needle. She twists and turns through the tight conduit, narrowly avoiding pipes and circuitry.

Two fighter crafts follow her inside and collide with the walls, showering the tunnel with blue sparks.

"Guys, is it just me or is the tunnel getting smaller?" asks Blendin.

Dipper looks up through a window on the top of the ship right before it collides with a pipe. "Yeah, it's definitely getting smaller!" he says. "SLOW DOWN, MABEL!"

Mabel eases back on the throttle.

They move at a leisurely pace through the narrow corridor.

It gets so tight that everyone has to help direct her.

"A little forward!" says Davy Time-Jones. "A little more!"

"We're clear on the back!" says Dipper.

"Just a little . . . STOP!" yells Blendin.

Mabel has wedged the spacecraft into the tightest part of the conduit. She tries reversing it and jamming it forward, but it won't go anywhere.

"We're stuck!" says Dipper.

"Dangit!" yells Mabel. "What happened?"

"Looks like they caught their design flaw and fixed it," says Blendin. "Huh, I guess they're not idiots!"

"So we're just stuck inside this enormous spacecraft?" says Dipper.

The gang pops open a ventilation hatch in the cockpit roof and peers out as Davy Time-Jones lights a match. The hallway isn't a hallway at all. It's a cellblock. Rows of prison cells line the walls.

"Wait a minute," says Dipper. "Did we just escape prison into another prison?"

"Well, technically it's called a brig, 'cause it's on a ship," says Davy. "But I won't split hairs. Unless we get bored, and then splitting hairs is a great way to pass the time."

"Hey, no need!" says Mabel, who's exploring a corner. "They have magazines here!" She fans out several issues as if they're playing cards in a deck.

"*Time Life, Time Time, Time Illustrated*," says Blendin. "Man, these are some top-notch choices!"

Even Chamillacles garbles sounds of enjoyment.

"Who wants to take the time-personality time quiz in *Time Cosmo*?" asks Mabel.

"Me! Me! Me!" says Davy Time-Jones, jumping up and down.

The group sits in a circle and takes personality quizzes.

They truly get to know themselves for the first time ever. Which is nice, but they're still in jail. Their quest for the Time Pirates' Treasure has finally reached its . . .

CONFRONT THE OUTLAWS IN THE SALOON

"**G**uys, I think it's time to clean up this old-timey town," says Dipper.

With a smug smile, Dipper approaches the swinging double doors of the saloon and throws them open.

A hush falls over the honky-tonk.

"My name's Pioneer Pines," he says, "and I'm looking for—"

SMACK!

The swinging doors rebound and collide with Dipper's back, causing him to stumble. He reaches for something to steady himself, but his hand finds only a tablecloth.

He pulls it to the ground and sarsaparilla bottles fall like dominoes around the bar until . . .

CRASH!

One shatters in the lap of a hulking monstrous bandit, who stops chewing his gum and slowly rises to his feet. His enormous belt buckle has an inscription reading WILD EYES JOE and a smaller cursive subheading reading THE MOST FEARED OUTLAW IN THE LAND. The room freezes with anticipation.

"Sorry!" squeaks out Dipper in his prepubescent kitten voice.

Wild Eyes Joe struts across the saloon and grabs Dipper by the collar. "These are my favorite chaps you just spilled on," he says, his wild eyes bulging from their sockets. "What manner o' fella comes in a place like this and spills sarsaparilla on a man's chaps?"

Dipper stammers incoherently. "We're looking for a—a—"

"Are you an outlaw?" says Wild Eyes Joe. "Some kinda *law*? Or just an idiot? 'Cause I don't take kindly to none of those," he snarls.

Dipper nearly faints from the smell of Wild Eyes Joe's breath.

"You better start explainin', or I'm gonna have a little conversation with my friend the undertaker!" says Wild Eyes Joe.

"Oooh! What about?" asks Mabel with a smile.

"ABOUT KILLING YOU!" he says.

Mabel gasps.

Dipper looks around.

There's an empty stage.

Maybe I could lie and tell him we're the new saloon entertainment, he thinks.

There's also an empty seat at the card table.

Or maybe I could play it cool and pretend I'm here for the game.

Either way, YOU better decide NOW!

SAY THEY'RE THE NEW ENTERTAINMENT: GO TO PAGE 173

SAY THEY'RE HERE TO PLAY CARDS: GO TO PAGE 196

NOT TO BE GREEDY

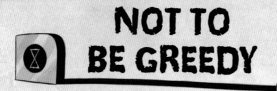

"**M**abel," says Dipper, "let's be sensible and call it quits."

Mabel nods.

"B-but—but—but—" stammers Blendin.

Mabel swats the time tape out of his hand.

Blendin sulks.

"So how do we get this all home?" asks Mabel.

"Well, I brought a few infinite sacks." Blendin produces what look like shiny silver trash bags. "These sacks exploit a loophole in space-time to give you infinite room!"

The twins and Blendin divide the treasure into equal thirds and fill up their sacks. They throw them over their shoulders and climb up through the time door, back into the time stream. Blendin navigates them to a spot that will drop them back in their own time.

"Thanks for the riches, Blendin!" says Mabel.

"Aw, shucks, you guys," says Blendin. "Finding this treasure is going to turn my life around once and for all. Thank *you*!" He pulls out his time phone, dials a number, and waits for someone to pick up. "Hello? Hello! Yes, Mother, it's me. And I have a little announcement to make. I'm moving out!" He clicks his heels. "Also, I'm never going to call my stepdad. So there!" Blendin grins from ear to ear as he hangs up the phone. Dipper and Mabel give him an enthusiastic thumbs-up. Unexpectedly, Blendin hugs the twins. He gets self-conscious and quickly steps back. "Sorry, guys. I guess it's just, in one thousand time lines, this is the only one where I've ever made . . . a friend."

"BOO!" says Dipper. Mabel elbows him in the gut.

"Anytime, Blar-Blar," says Mabel, smiling. "Anytime."

✦ ✦✦ ✦

It's twilight in Gravity Falls. Fireflies are coming out and the nighttime air is humming as Dipper and Mabel drag their sacks of treasure home.

"Man, this sure is getting heavy," says Mabel, sweating.

"Can't stop . . . Almost home . . . Almost rich," says Dipper.

Mabel pauses and leans against her treasure sack. "You know, Dipper, I've been thinking. If one little choice like which sweater to wear could get us infinite treasure, what kind of impact is having infinite treasure gonna have on our lives?"

Dipper wipes his brow. "Man, a lot of people are gonna want a piece of this. And there's probably going to be taxes to be paid and investment decisions to be made. Grunkle Stan's going to want a cut. We'll have to decide whether to give him some. Oof, it's like the richer we are, the more choices we have to make."

"Maybe it's just me," says Mabel, "but after spending a whole day choosing and choosing, I could honestly go for never making another choice again."

"Wanna bury these in the woods and forget about the whole thing for now?" asks Dipper.

"Absolutely," says Mabel.

So Dipper and Mabel dig a hole, bury their sacks of treasure, and dust off their hands. It's not a total loss, though. Dipper keeps one gold coin, because one coin has the power, when flipped, to make a decision *for* them, and they won't have to stress about making choices ever again.

"Wanna go watch the new episode of *Duck-tective*?" asks Mabel, checking her watch.

Dipper flips the coin and smiles. "Absolutely. We're right on time."

Laughing, they run back to the Mystery Shack for . . .

 THE ONE TRUE END.

Congratulations, dear reader. You've chosen wisely. But did you find a secret . . . ?

JUMP THE JUMP

"**L**et's JUMP IT!" says Mabel, steering the space racer toward the depression. "I am *over*confident in my skills and *under*confident in Blendin's death warnings. This should be perfect!" Mabel uses the racer's dwindling power to speed toward the hole.

Dipper digs his fingernails into the armrests.

"All right, here goes . . . CUTTING THROTTLE!" Mabel screams. She throttles back and they slide into the pit.

Dipper turns green.

Even without the jet propulsion, the space racer is gaining speed as it careens down the canyon wall. Then the racer begins to spiral toward the bottom.

"Careful . . . careful . . . you have to time this just right!" says Blendin over the intercom.

"Three . . . two . . . NOW!" Mabel yells. She jams the throttle to its maximum.

The space racer accelerates forward with its last bit of energy.

It's climbing the wall.

It's racing forward at breakneck speed.

The twins hold on as they launch out of the gap and soar through the air.

"It's working!" shouts Mabel.

"We're passing *Racer T*!" yells Dipper.

"You're passing everyone!" says Blendin through the intercom.

But . . . they're still rising in altitude. Suddenly, their instruments go haywire. The world starts flickering around them. There are flashes of light—

VKDSHV DQG FRORUV ZKLC SDVW! WLPH LWVHOI VHHPV WR VORZ WR D FUDZO! EOHQGLQ VFUHDPV! ZKHUH DUH WKHB JRLQJ?!

 ZZZ.GLVQHBAG.FRP/DZURQJWXUQ

MABEL TALKS

"**Dipper, this is the sort of situation** that requires finesse, charm, and general Mabel-iness," says Mabel before trotting Black-Spirit-Beauty-Biscuit up to the train. "PEOPLE OF THE *CALAMITY LIMITED*!" she shouts. "Sorry for the trouble! We're not here to hurt you or your fabulous topcoats and corsets! All we seek is a simple object one of you might possess. Do we have your permission to board the train and discuss this?" Mabel surveys the crowd. "Potentially over tea and scones?"

The passengers look at one another, slowly nodding

"We don't see why not!" yells back one passenger.

"To be honest, that sounds lovely!" yells another.

"Thank you very much, you wonderful angels!" says Mabel before boarding the train with Dipper and Blendin.

Mabel walks down the aisle of the train. She makes a point of complimenting as many passengers as she can. "Hello! Hey, there! Ooooh, look at your mustache! What fine bonnets you have! Is that a bustle? WHAAAAT?" she says.

The passengers smile at Mabel as she passes.

A little boy runs up to her. "Mrs. Bandit Lady, will you please take my daddy's watch?"

Another kid runs up and pushes his way between the little boy and Mabel. "Take *my* daddy's watch!" he says.

"Consarn both of you! Take *my* watch!" screams a man.

"Guys, guys, calm down!" says Mabel. "I don't want any

of your valuables except for this key!" Mabel unfurls the illustrated treasure map and shows them the Time Key.

Everyone nods.

One man steps forward. "I know of the key you seek!" he says. "A man in frilly frocks with clocks in his beard came on board this train. Before he disappeared, he spoke to me of such a key and said that he was worried that it might be haunted, so he sold it to someone in town. Can't remember to whom, exactly. Back in town is the key!"

"Awww, sassafras," says Mabel, turning to leave.

"Wait, don't go!" calls out the man.

"Yeah, stay! Stay with us!" says a passenger. "We've never met such a polite and charming bandit!"

"Awww, I appreciate it, guys, but I really need to find that key!" says Mabel.

"Come on, just stay for one sarsaparilla?" begs the boy. "It's a weird old-timey root drink that we inexplicably love!"

Mabel looks at Dipper.

Dipper shakes his head.

Mabel looks back at all the passengers' smiling faces.

A little girl tugs on Mabel's skirt.

"Oh, man. What should I do?" asks Mabel.

STAY FOR SARSAPARILLAS: GO TO PAGE 193

POLITELY DECLINE AND GO BACK TO TOWN: GO TO PAGE 259

TIME DUKES

"**W**e roll with the Time Dukes!" says Dipper.

"That's fantastic!" says Davy Time-Jones.

Dipper, Mabel, and Blendin let out big sighs.

"Because it means I get to enjoy beating you to a pulp!" Davy Time-Jones lifts up his eye patch to reveal a clock for an eye that reads CLOCK KINGS 4 LYF.

"Oh, man," says Dipper. He ducks and dodges a bowlful of hot chili.

The twins grab whatever they can and hurl it back at the Time Pirate. Mabel throws a handful of uncooked broccoli; Dipper tosses a slice of ham. Both hit Davy Time-Jones in the face.

Davy Time-Jones clenches his fists and trembles with

rage. "CLOCK KINGS! ASSEMBLE! TAKE OUT THESE PUNY TIME DUKES!"

All the other Clock Kings drop what they're doing and surround Blendin and the twins. Suddenly, there's a laser blast and everyone gets quiet. Standing on a balcony is the warden, with a smoking weapon in his hand. Everyone freezes.

"Now, y'all know I like to keep this Infinitentiary in order," says the warden. "Fella steps outta line, I got no problem with de-aging him using my reverse chrono-blaster. Yah!" The warden whips out his chrono-blaster and points it at a bearded elderly convict.

Immediately, the convict reverse-ages, getting younger and younger until he is just a gurgling baby rolling around in a prison jumpsuit. Everyone gasps.

"So unless y'all want to be infantilized right now, I suggest you turn in whoever started this here fight," says the warden.

One hundred convict fingers point at Dipper, Mabel, and Blendin.

The baby lets out a long wail.

"How would you three bad apples like to spend some time in solitary confinement?" asks the warden.

"Oooh, an upgrade!" says Mabel.

"Not exactly," says the warden, appearing beside them on the cafeteria floor. Pointing his chrono-blaster at them, he leads them into the dark of the prison, throws them in a single cell, and locks them away.

"Wait, are we actually stuck in prison for life now?" asks Mabel.

"Yes, we are," says Blendin. "But . . . there's a fun game I personally invented called Scratch the Days into the Wall! What you do is you take a stone and scratch a line into the wall," adds Blendin as he does it. "There, that's one, that's for today. Now, we just do this again tomorrow and, well . . . every day for the rest of our lives. Wanna play it with me? It's a totally original game that only I know about!"

"No," says Mabel. "I'm good."

"Should have said 'Clock Kings,'" mutters Dipper, scratching a line into the wall.

For the trio, it looks like it's . . .

 **THE END.**

GIVE DOS HUNTHOU TO SOMEONE IN NEED

"**All right, I'm just gonna say** what everyone is thinking and point out that this guy smells . . . not great," says Mabel. "I vote we turn him over to someone in need."

"I agree," says Dipper.

"Me three," says Blendin.

"Then it's settled. But who do we know that could use a servant?" asks Mabel.

Blendin gets a phone call and picks up. "Hey, Mom!" he says. "NO. No, I haven't picked up any time cats yet. NO. I'm out with friends, Mom. No, they're not imaginary friends, they're real this time! NO, I can't help you with that. I'm busy, okay? Get off my time-back!"

Blendin hangs up the phone. "Sorry about that, you guys. Sometimes my mom calls, and, like, she's really demanding. If only there were two of me, then I could meet all her requests, and then I wouldn't have to hunt for this stupid treasure."

Dipper and Mabel look at each other.

"Well, this presents an oddly convenient solution," says Dipper.

Mabel nods in agreement. "Mr. Hunthou," she says, "we've found a master for you to serve: Blendin!"

Blendin's jaw drops. "M-m-m-m-m-m-m-m-me? Really, you guys?" he says.

"Yeah, I really think you could turn each other's lives around," says Mabel. "He can help you with your mom, and you can try to teach him how to have a life outside of serving people. Maybe you can get an apartment together and turn it into a reality TV show! Plus, I'm kind of over treasure hunting. I could really go for some TV right now."

"Yeah, TV is pretty great," says Dipper. "Welp, enjoy your life, Blendin!"

"Thank you guys so much. This is gonna change everything!" He gives Dipper and Mabel an enormous hug.

"Please never touch us again," says Dipper.

"Agreed!" says Mabel.

Dipper and Mabel grab the time tape. They take one

last look at Blendin, who's asking Dos Hunthou if he wants to play catch. Dos Hunthou does. Blendin is so happy he clicks his heels.

"Well, we've still got the key!" says Dipper. "Want to get that time treasure?"

"Wait, where did the key go?" asks Mabel.

"I thought you had it!" says Dipper.

They both turn to see that while they were talking, a slobbering alien possum creature grabbed the key and scampered away into the crowd.

"Dang it!" says Mabel. "Well, we didn't get any treasure, but I think this was a rewarding experience."

"Probably not as rewarding as the Time Pirates' Treasure, though," groans Dipper.

"Definitely not," says Mabel.

They pull the time tape and go home.

 **THE END**

EMBARK ON A MINING ADVENTURE

"**Ooooh, oh, oh, I wanna go to the mine,**" says Blendin. "I've always dreamt of being a miner! Days spent beneath the earth! Talking to moles! Working with your hands!"

Mabel pats Blendin on the shoulder. "What a strange man you are," she says with a smile.

"Well, hopefully the prospector in the mine has the Time Key!" says Dipper.

The group loads up pack mules and heads out of town.

A dry wind stirs the air as they approach the mine in silence.

The place looks abandoned.

"It's sure nice out here," says Dipper. "You know, before traffic and screeching technology, you could really just take in the silen—"

BLAM!

The mules startle at the sound of a gunshot.

They take cover behind a rock.

In the entrance to the mine, a wily old prospector with a long beard and floppy hat emerges from the shadows holding a six-shooter. He looks very familiar. . . .

"Old Man McGucket?" asks Dipper.

"Naw, my name is Jugsley!" screeches the prospector in a voice almost identical to McGucket's. "But we hillbilly types all look mighty alike, so I don't blame ya for the mistake!" He peers at them skeptically. "Who are ye? Claim jumpers? Panhandlers? Armadillos dressed up in man-clothes?" He fires into the air again, then dances a wild jig and makes nonsensical hooting sounds.

Blendin and Dipper look at each other.

Mabel steps forward. "Hi, there. Mabel here," she says. "First let me say your hat looks amazing."

The prospector lowers the weapon. "I'm listening," he says.

"We're not claim jumpers, we promise," she says. "We have no interest in taking any of your gold or silver . . . or . . ." She looks around. "What do you mine here?"

"Boron!" he says, slapping his knee.

"Right. We definitely want none of whatever that is," says Mabel. "We're looking for a key. A worthless old key that some friends told us may have been traded to you."

The prospector gives them a discerning look.

"Why, that's right . . . did the man happen to wear all manner of puffy flamboyant clothing, and a beard with clocks in it?"

"Yup!" Mabel says to Jugsley. "Sounds about right!"

"Well, flapjack my haystack!" he says. "Such a fellow came in here and traded me the key you seek! Come on in!" Jugsley leads them inside the boron mine. There are piles of clothes, pocket watches, and hats in all sizes and shapes.

"Something looks very suspicious about all this," Blendin whispers to the twins.

"Yeah, where did all this stuff come from?" Mabel whispers.

"And what happened to its owners?" whispers Dipper. "Come to notice it, Jugsley seems to be blinking and involuntarily swallowing a lot."

Blendin grips Dipper and Mabel. "Time to go," he whispers.

The twins exchange glances.

Jugsley has led them to a fork in the mine. "The key you're looking for is right down there in that dark, foreboding pit," he says. He gestures to a short tunnel ending in a pit.

Dipper and Mabel gulp.

"Are you sure about that?" asks Dipper. "Wouldn't you rather have us go down that other tunnel? You know . . . the one with bright lanterns that looks like it actually goes somewhere?"

The prospector grins with wild eyes. "Nope," he says. "Go down the one on the right. Ain't nothing bad ever happened to no one who went down there! Ignore all them human-looking booooones!" He lets out a cackle and licks his lips.

The friends squeeze together into a huddle.

"Guys, this horrifying whack job is the dictionary definition of *untrustworthy*," says Dipper. "He's probably going to knock us out with a pickax and steal our stuff or something."

"Yeah, he gives me the willies," says Blendin. "And I would know! In high school, I was voted most likely to give strangers the willies!"

"C'mon, guys, if I've learned anything out here, it's that you should never make the obvious choice," says Mabel.

"Should we trust this maniac or insist on going the other way?" asks Blendin.

Well? What should they do?!

TRUST THE PROSPECTOR: GO TO PAGE 232

GO THE OTHER WAY: GO TO PAGE 58

POLITELY DECLINE AND GO BACK TO TOWN

Dipper shoots Mabel a stern glance.

Mabel sighs. "All right," she says. "I'm sorry, everyone, but I really need to go!"

"Awww, don't leave us!" says one passenger. "We are ever so charmed by your cheerful demeanor!"

"At the very least, take a souvenir to remember us by!" says a small gap-toothed child. "Like my hat!"

"Heh, uh, sure. Of course!" says Mabel.

"Yeah, and take my pickax!" says a grubby, wild-eyed prospector.

"And some of my pies!" says a pie maker.

"And my six-shooter that's free of fingerprints!" adds a passenger wearing all black, his eyes darting suspiciously.

One by one, all the passengers give Mabel a token to remember them by, and by the time she's left the train, she's carrying a huge heavy satchel filled with souvenirs. They make their way toward the town. Just outside of it, Mabel stops and drops the satchel.

"Guys, I dunno how long I can carry this," she says.

"Good. Then how about we throw it away?" says Dipper.

"What? Never!" exclaims Mabel. "Each souvenir is a

symbol of love! And there are some moths in this bag that I've already given names to!"

Dipper groans.

"Hey, hey, hey, there's another solution!" says Blendin. "I can open up a *time cache*." He changes the settings on one of his laser guns and blasts open a portal. He takes the gift satchel and tosses it in.

"Whoa, what's that?" asks Mabel.

"It's like storage space. You can store matter in the space in between various time lines," Blendin explains.

"Like the way Grunkle Stan hides money in the walls!" says Mabel.

"Or the way Lazy Susan hides bacon in her pie crusts!" adds Dipper.

"Let's put our bandit disguises in there for safe keeping in case we need them again!" Mabel tosses in her bandana and mustache and watches them float into the space.

Dipper and Blendin do the same with their mustaches and bandanas.

"So, can we just retrieve all our stuff later?" asks Dipper.

"Yes!" exclaims Blendin. "Except . . . except . . . ah, jeez." Blendin adjusts the knobs on his laser blaster. "All right, small problem. I may have forgotten to program coordinates, so . . . that stuff is lost forever."

"What?" yells Mabel, frowning. "My precious treasures!"

"Yeah, I kinda really screwed this one up," says Blendin. "How about we just go back to town and pet some farm animals?"

Mabel stares at Blendin. "You're lucky I like baby goats," she says through gritted teeth.

"I wonder what's gonna happen to all that stuff," says Dipper.

"Oh, I don't know. It'll probably float through the ether of space-time like a bottle in the ocean, wandering hopelessly till it washes up on the time shores of some time beach," says Blendin. He gives Mabel a pat on the back.

"Good-bye, friends!" she says to the empty space where the portal used to be.

They wander into town.

"Well, what should we do now?" asks Mabel. "I'm open to anything as long as I get to keep making new old-timey friends!"

CONFRONT THE OUTLAWS IN THE SALOON: GO TO PAGE 237

EMBARK ON A MINING ADVENTURE: GO TO PAGE 255

LEAVE BLENDIN BEHIND

"**M**abel, this has gone on too long." Dipper smacks a fist into his palm. "Also, *Duck-tective* is coming back from hiatus and I don't want to miss it," he says as he walks across the sand to a spot beneath the time door.

"I guess you're right," says Mabel. "Sorry, Blendin! Thanks for the fun day, though!"

Blendin looks crestfallen as the Time Pirates cackle, drag him aboard their galleon, and begin to ready the plank.

Dipper helps Mabel climb up through the time door and then follows her off the beach and back into the fourth-dimensional in-between space.

"Well, I feel good about that decision," says Dipper as he dusts off his hands. "Now, uh . . . how do we get back to our own time?"

"You mean you don't know how?" asks Mabel. "Ugh, I knew we should have done the right thing." She kicks the wall of flowing time in anger.

The time stream sucks the shoe right off her foot.

"Ugh! And now my favorite shoe is lost in the antebellum South," she says.

Dipper is poking around the time walls. "I mean, I think if we can find our time, we can just leap through the wall into it. There's gotta be something around here somewhere."

Mabel is searching, too. "Like here! I think I hear Grunkle Stan!" she says.

"Yeah, this will probably work," says Dipper. He walks up to double-check, but Mabel trips over her remaining shoe and they both fall out of the time stream and tumble into . . . aristocratic France.

The twins are inside a glittering mansion in the 1700s.

"*Quelle domage!*" screams a powder-wigged man.

"*Mon dieu!*" screams his wife.

The panicked couple runs away from the twins, leaving Dipper and Mabel alone in a room filled with fancy cheeses. Dipper and Mabel sample them.

"Wow, these are really good," says Mabel.

"Tell me about it!" says Dipper.

"We sure picked a good place to get lost forever," she says.

"Mmmmm-hmmmm!" says Dipper through a mouthful of cheese.

✦ ✦✦ ✦

The twins eventually learn to speak French and live out the rest of their lives as aristocrats . . . until they're on the wrong side of a revolution and it basically turns into that famous French story about the miserable people. You know, the one with songs and peasants, and it's all about the miserables. I think it's called *The Miserables*.

 THE END

BUY THE LESSER RACER

"**Y**ou know what, Dipper?** Let's not take our chances," says Mabel, putting her hand over the probability square. "I'm having a bad hair day and that usually means it's also a bad luck day."

Blendin lets out a huge sigh.

"I guess we can make do with the junky racer," says Dipper.

"Well, the part of me that lives for the thrill of gambling is plumb sad to hear you say that!" says Glorglax Gleeful. "But the part of me that wants my customers to leave happy is all right! The part of me that is cyborg is neutral." The sales-borg pulls a sheet off a much junkier, rusted-out, dust-blasted space racer. Possum-like alien creatures skitter out of it. "It doesn't have puncture-proof fuel tanks, but it'll do. I'll draw up the paperwork and arrange to have this sent to the races. Who's paying for it?"

The twins push Blendin forward. "That's on this guy!" says Dipper.

Mabel leans toward Blendin to whisper, "Don't worry, we're gonna get your money back."

"We win a lot," says Dipper. "You're on the heroes' side now."

Blendin stumbles into the signing office.

✦ ✦ ✦

"LADIES AND GENTLE-BORGS, PUT YOUR VARIOUS DISGUSTING APPENDAGES TOGETHER FOR THE 20705 SPACE CAPSULE RACES, SPONSORED BY PITT COLA EXTREME BLAST: THE SODA THAT IS SENTIENT AND FEELS PAIN WHEN YOU DRINK IT!"

The roar of a hundred thousand creatures from all across the galaxy shakes the ground as the twins enter the arena. In the mouth of an enormous canyon hover fifty space capsules glistening beneath the hot midday sun. Racers are busy making final adjustments to their vehicles.

Blendin runs up to the twins. "All right," he says, "so I've entered us into the race and struck a deal with Emperor Snorgshnog, the current owner of Dos Hunthou. If we win, then he'll free Dos Hunthou, who'll be able to tell us where to find the Time Key, but if we lose, we'll have to wear metal bikinis in his space casino for the rest of our lives! Which

I would argue isn't that empowering!" Blendin motions toward Emperor Snorgshnog, who watches through opera glasses from a private hovering balcony.

Beside the emperor, with a shackle around his neck, is a ragged, shirtless bald man with an enormous hourglass-shaped scar across his face. He breathes erratically, like a chained animal. Carved on his neck shackle is the name DOS HUNTHOU.

"Man, the future is a weird place," says Dipper. "And I really wish my soda would stop screaming at me." He pours out his shrieking Pitt Cola as he grabs a racing helmet and starts to get in the space racer.

"Whoa, whoa, whoa," says Mabel. "What makes you think you're driving?"

"What?" says Dipper. "Mabel, I beat you in racing games every time. Plus, I don't start dancing when Sev'ral Timez comes on the car radio."

"Pssssh, you trippin'! This is clearly a Mabel job," she says, putting on a helmet. "Who's better at riding bikes?"

"Hey, that wasn't my fault! I just have short legs and couldn't reach the pedals!" says Dipper.

"GUYS! The race is about to start. You need to pick a pilot!" calls Blendin.

The twins look at him.

"How about you pick?" Dipper asks.

"Ah, jeez . . ." says Blendin. "Uhh . . . uhhh . . ."

DIPPER DRIVES: GO TO PAGE 117

MABEL DRIVES: GO TO PAGE 108

BLOCK THE PATH

"**I**'m feeling irrationally confident!" says Dipper. "Gimme a laser blaster!"

Blendin tosses one laser blaster to Mabel and one to Dipper, who catches it, twirls it around his finger, and then takes a shot at the rocks above the tunnel.

BLAM!

A glowing blue ball of energy fires from the blaster and careens toward the rocks, hitting them dead-on. The rocks explode like fireworks and cascade down the cliff face to block the path. The engineer quickly pulls the brake, and the enormous train screeches and starts to slow.

"Nailed it," says Dipper before realizing the laser blaster is burning hot. "Ah, hot-hot-hot!" he yelps, juggling the red-hot weapon and sucking his thumb.

The train reaches a full stop and Mabel shoots her laser blaster into the air to grab the passengers' attention. Passengers crowd the windows. Peering at Dipper, Mabel, and Blendin, they clutch each other and shiver. Some passengers even start whimpering.

"Uh, what do we do now?" asks Dipper. "Should I talk? Do you want to talk?"

"I don't know! I didn't think this far ahead!" says Mabel. "Say something!"

"No, you say something!" he says.

"Guys, I'll say something!" says Blendin.

Mabel looks at him and says, "Awww, I think the adults should handle this one." She motions to herself and Dipper. "So who's it gonna be, Dipper? We're starting to lose our audience!"

"Uhhh . . . uhhhhh . . ." says Dipper.

DIPPER TALKS: GO TO PAGE 78

MABEL TALKS: GO TO PAGE 247

FIND OUT WHAT THE CROWD THINKS

Dipper, **Mabel, and Blendin** watch forty hands reach for weapons.

"WOOO-HOOO!" screams the crowd, everyone firing wildly into the air.

Wild Eyes Joe approaches the stage.

"Kids, that's the best gosh-darn show I've ever seen in my life," he says. "Here, have some money!" He beams and hands Dipper an old-timey Union banknote. There's an image of an eagle being shot out of a cannon and a scroll reading CARPETBAGGER'S BURDEN. "Everybody, give these kids some money!"

The whole crowd showers the stage with bills and coins.

"Will you perform again?" asks Wild Eyes Joe.

Dipper and Mabel look at each other.

"Dipper," says Mabel from the side of her mouth, "we have a mission here, remember? We have to see if these outlaws have the Time Key."

"YES! YES, YES, YES!" yells Blendin as he catches bills. He leans toward the twins and whispers, "I've never received this much praise in my entire life. You have to help me do it again!"

Dipper looks to Mabel and shrugs. "I don't see why not," he says. "I mean, they *are* showering us with money! And this nickel has an image of a winking muskrat on it!"

They take it from the top and run through the number a second time.

The crowd goes wild.

"Shouldn't we get going?" asks Mabel after their tenth performance. "My legs are sore from hoedown fatigue."

Dipper looks at Blendin, who's smiling from ear to ear. "I dunno, Mabel," he says. "Blendin seems . . . really happy. Maybe for the first time in his entire life. What if he's better off here in the West as a weird vaudeville entertainer?"

"Guys, I thought treasure was gonna fix my life, but I've found something better: praise from toothless criminals," says Blendin. "Here, take my time tape and money and go home!" Blendin shoves the time tape and the cash from the outlaws into the twins' hands.

"Yay. Ten dollars," says Mabel with a frown.

"I'll read about you in the history books," says Dipper to Blendin. "I mean, that is, if you haven't completely altered time by being here," he adds with a laugh. "But what's the worst that could happen?"

With a nod, the twins pull the tape and return to the Mystery Shack. They find Grunkle Stan sitting on the couch watching TV as usual.

"Where have you kids been?" Grunkle Stan asks.

"If we told you, you wouldn't even believe us," says Dipper with a smirk.

"Really? Try me," says Stan. "And by try me, I really mean *ZRSKRUAD SLKDH SDUIFH HVEE SCRUK SHDOIS*

SNARGHHH CHAAAAAAAA!" Stan screams as he rips off his mask, revealing a horrible reptilian head beneath.

The twins shout.

It's too late.

The future is ruled by lizard-faced reptoids.

Way to go, reader.
In all honesty, the kids should have seen this coming.

 **THE END**

CLOCK KINGS

"**W**e're affiliated with the Clock Kings!" says Dipper.

Davy Time-Jones stares at him. "BROTHER!" he yells. He embraces both Blendin and the twins with one of his enormous arms. "We could always use more Clock Kings. You're gonna be thrilled to see this." He lifts up his eye patch to reveal he has a clock for an eye, and it's engraved with the words CLOCK KINGS 4 LYF.

"Oooh, that's nice," says Blendin.

"Shiny!" says Mabel.

"What purpose could that possibly serve?" asks Dipper. Mabel elbows him in the gut.

"I was worried I was gonna have to take y'all down," says Davy Time-Jones, "but now that I know I can trust y'all with my life, what say you help me give these Time Dukes what for?" He throws a fist in the air. "IT'S TIME FOR THE FOOD FIGHT OF OUR LIVES!"

Dipper, Mabel, and Blendin shrug, then follow him into battle. They grab whatever food they can find and start flinging it at the Time Dukes. Fellow Clock Kings rush to help them out. One even dives and takes a face full of mustard for Mabel.

"Wow," says Mabel. "Who knew you could get so much friendship mileage out of pretending to like the same things as someone?"

With the help of the twins and Blendin, Davy Time-Jones beats back the Time Dukes in a stunning victory before the prison guards break up the riot. One of the guards shoots a Time Duke with a reverse-aging chrono-blaster, transforming him into a baby before their very eyes. The Clock Kings laugh and high-five.

Davy Time-Jones beams at Dipper, Mabel, and Blendin. "Brothers, I am mighty impressed with your food-rioting skills," he says. "What are your names?"

"I'm Dipper Pines and this is my twin sister, Mabel," says Dipper. "And this is Blar-Blar. I mean, Blendin."

"Nice to meet you three!" says Davy Time-Jones. "I think you'd make fine accomplices to a little project me and our fellow Clock Kings are working on." He leans toward them. "At midnight, make sure you're packed and ready to go," he whispers before heading off to his cell.

Mabel turns to Blendin. "Uh, what was that all about?" she asks.

"Don't you see?" whispers Blendin. "He and his boys are staging a prison breakout, and they've invited us to participate!" He grins. "This is the first time I've been invited to participate in anything!"

A guard locks the twins and Blendin in their cell.

"We've earned his trust now!" Blendin whispers. "We're basically almost Time Pirates ourselves!"

"And hopefully if we help him break out, he'll tell us about the Time Key!" says Dipper.

The three high-five and then rest up before the big break.

✦ ✦✦ ✦

At midnight, the cellblock is silent.

A guard whistles and drags his nightstick-saber along the glowing cell bars.

The twins and Blendin sit awake, holding their breath.

"What's keeping these guys?" whispers Mabel.

They hear the sounds of a scuffle, and they see the guard unholster his chrono-blaster and peer down a hallway. Suddenly, an enormous tongue lashes out of nowhere and snatches him. The twins only hear his scream, followed by the crunch of his bones. A moment later, Davy Time-Jones and the anthropomorphic chameleon stroll up with the guard's keys and open their cell.

"Brothers, this is Chamillacles," says Davy Time-Jones, introducing the chameleon. "He's great at blending in, as well as shedding his skin, which is really gross, so you should just ignore that. He only speaks Gleep-Glorp, though, so anything you want to say to him, I'll have to translate. Anyway, let's go, Clock Kings! I've got a getaway car waiting!"

The twins and Blendin rush out of the cell, but just as they do, they notice the guard has managed to crawl toward the door and reach for the alarm button.

Chamillacles swats the guard's hand away with his long tongue, but it's too late.

RRRRRRRR! RRRRRRRR! RRRRRRRR!

The alarm screeches, and the entire prison is bathed in red flashing lights.

Through a window, the gang spots a space cruiser speeding away from the building.

"Our getaway car!" yells Davy Time-Jones. "It's getting away! What do we do now?"

A guard charges at them, but Chamillacles catches him with a quick lash of the tongue. He propels the guard into Davy Time-Jones's fist.

BLAM!

Three more guards run in and draw their lasers.

Davy and Chamillacles bash the guards' heads together, knocking them out cold.

Dipper looks at the unconscious guards. "Guys!" he says. "What if we take their uniforms and pretend we're guards? I've seen that work out in a lot of movies!"

"The guards have a teleportation system on and off the prison. We could just use that!" says Davy Time-Jones.

Mabel, who's swiped a map off one of the guard's

waists, points out a nearby room labeled ESCAPE SHIPS. "Or," she says, "what if we steal one of those bad boys and fly it back to Earth?"

"I'd like to say, I'm just happy to be participating!" yells Blendin.

Everyone ignores him.

Davy Time-Jones looks to the twins. "What do you think we should do, brothers? CLOCK KINGS FOR LIFE!"

DRESS UP AS GUARDS TO ESCAPE: GO TO PAGE 26

STEAL A SPACESHIP: GO TO PAGE 203

TAKE OUT THE BRIDGE

"**I**'m sorry, Mr. Lobster General!" says Mabel. "But we're gonna have to take you down!" She steers their ship toward the massive spacecraft.

Dipper fires the onboard laser, destroying a swarm of incoming droid bots. "Now!" he yells.

Mabel flips open a switch cover and mashes a glowing red button.

The fuel tanks soar toward the bridge, seemingly in slow motion.

"*Gleem glom glor glom glee glee!*" says Chamillacles.

"He's saying we'll have thirty seconds to get away from the ship before the boosters hit it and explode!" says Davy Time-Jones. "But it took ten seconds for me to explain that, and another five seconds for me to explain this, so that means we have fifteen seconds right now, I repeat, ten seconds!"

"Enough math!" Mabel shouts. She fires up the thrusters and they speed away as the ship explodes behind them! Clocks and dodos and knights and cowboys burst out of the explosion. A *T. rex* floats gracefully past their window, wiggling its tiny little arms.

"Whoa, why did that happen?" asks Dipper.

"These spaceships use time fuel!" says Blendin. "Therefore, we caused a time explosion!"

Everyone nods.

"Yeah, that makes sense," says Mabel with a smile.

"No, time explosions are a bad thing!" screams Blendin. "The *Titanic* is floating our way!"

"Don't worry," says Mabel. "I read half of a book about the *Titanic* and I know that everything works out fine for those guys!"

Suddenly, the *Titanic* CRASHES into their ship!

What are the odds?

For our heroes, it looks like . . .

THE END.

 SURRENDER

"**B**lendin, give me one of your blasters!" Dipper shouts.

Blendin tosses one to him, and Dipper activates it and puts his finger on the trigger, causing the lawmen to freeze.

Mabel sighs. "Dipper, wait! What are we gonna do, spend the rest of our lives as outlaws?" she asks.

Dipper scratches his chin. "I'm open to it," he says.

"It beats living with my mom," says Blendin.

Mabel shakes her head. "We should turn ourselves in. It's the right thing to do. Also, riding a horse hurts my butt."

"Aw, all right," says Dipper. He powers down the blaster.

With heavy sighs, Dipper, Mabel, and Blendin put up their hands.

The sheriff and his crew pounce and cuff them.

"Well, hooooey! Looks like we caught ourselves a posse of regular old bandits," says the sheriff while dancing a jig and slapping his spurs. "You three have caused a *lot* of problems. Looks like y'all are gonna be in jail for a while!"

The lawmen throw them in the back of a stagecoach and drive it toward town.

As Blendin sulks in the back of the stagecoach, Dipper and Mabel shimmy toward the front, where the sheriff sits and whittles casually.

"So, uh, Mr. Sheriff, what's our punishment?" asks Mabel.

"Train-nappin'?" he asks. "Well, if it were up to me, I'd make y'all dress up like little trains and walk through town, and when someone tried to rob you, I wouldn't stop them. See how you like it. But I'm a touch odd in the head, so they don't let me choose punishments no more."

"Well, who does decide the punishments?" asks Dipper.

"Judge Hangamanforanycrime," says the sheriff. "And I warn you, he lives up to his name. He is an actual judge."

Dipper and Mabel tremble.

"He's only let a criminal off once," says the sheriff, "and it was on account of him being a child!"

"But *we're* children!" shouts Dipper.

"What, you three bloodthirsty ne'er-do-wells?" The sheriff laughs. "You're clearly adults who are just short on account of the malnutrition that's so popular in these times."

"It's true!" yells Mabel, taking off her bandana and mustache. "Look long and hard at me and my brother here!"

Dipper rips off his disguise.

The sheriff squints at them. "Well, I'll be hoodwinked. You *are* children! Hmmmm . . ." He pulls out a key and sets them free. He pauses when he gets to Blendin.

"I'm a child . . . too?" says Blendin, peeling off his mustache.

"You look like the biggest baby here," says the sheriff. "Plus, I reckon the townsfolk of Calamity Junction wouldn't get much satisfaction out of usin' capital punishment on children. How about we let this go and, say, give you a second chance?"

"Really? Is there a catch?" asks Dipper.

"The catch is do it before I change my mind!" says the sheriff.

Dipper, Mabel, and Blendin spring to their feet.

"Thank you so much. We are soooo sorry," says Dipper.

"Seriously, so, so sorry!" says Mabel, dusting herself off.

They race the short distance into town, wiping their brows in relief and exchanging smiles.

"Well, now that we've got out of that all right, what should we do next?" asks Mabel.

"Looks like we should explore one of those other options if we're ever going to find this Time Key," says Blendin.

CONFRONT THE OUTLAWS IN THE SALOON: GO TO PAGE 237

EMBARK ON A MINING ADVENTURE: GO TO PAGE 255

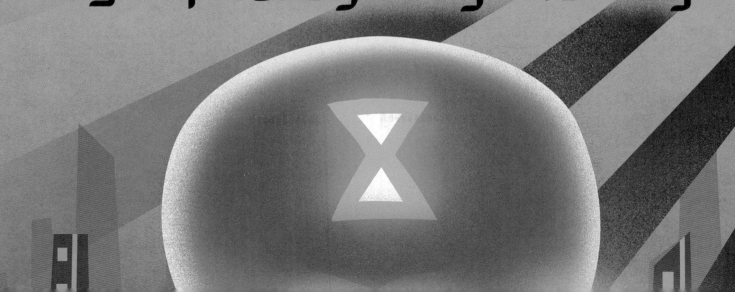